INTO HIS DARKNESS

Ashton Turriff

Copyright © 2022 by Ashton Turriff

All rights reserved.

No portion of this book may be reproduced in any form without written permission from the publisher or author, except as permitted by U.S. copyright law.

Contents

1. Trapped — 1
2. By His Darkness — 9
3. Monster — 18
4. Do You Remember: Part 1 — 22
5. Do you Remember: Part 2 — 28
6. Wolves Part 1 — 32
7. Wolves Part 2 — 36
8. If I Were King — 39
9. Coffee — 43
10. Dreaming of the future — 50
11. Drawing Close — 53
12. Without Warning — 60
13. Fire — 67
14. Feelings — 74
15. Jealousy — 80

16.	Warning	84
17.	Punishment For Your Betrayal	88
18.	Dancing? Rebellion?	93
19.	The Royal Hunt	101
20.	The Prey Part 1	106
21.	The Prey Part 2	110
22.	The Prey part 3	112
23.	Brother Against Brother	117

Chapter 1
Trapped

Ivy's POV

The day started like any other, I woke up early to feed the chickens and animals on my family's farm. It was my chores every day. If I didn't do my chores, or I was late on doing them; my parents would beat me. My father never raised his voice, it was always my mother beating me. My father has never raised his hand to me. He would always just give me a death stare and I knew I was in trouble. My mother felt like men don't know their strength so it was always up to her.

I always love looking after and taking care of the horse, they looked wild and free. I wish I could take a horse and a few of my things, never look back. Then I would be free. I would want Damian to come with me. We have been childhood lovers since long as I can remember. He's very sweet and very kind, their farm is next to ours. If we were to marry then, our families could have one big farm instead of two smaller farms. Of course, we would want our own land. We could trade some live stock for more land. Damian and I could have a great life together.

The day was almost done, after I finish brushing the horses I can go inside and have dinner. Only a few more hours of daylight. I wonder if my mother made her potato stew, it tastes even better from a hard day's work dealing with all the animals and doing things around the farm.

Brushing one of the horses, my mind snapped out of daydreaming when the king's knights stopped in front of our wooden fence of our farm. My father stopped what he was doing, "Welcome to our farm. Your highness."

"It's a small farm." "Yes, your highness."

My father bowed, then the man he was talking to walked out of the carriage. I looked around even my mother was bowing. "You crazy girl, bow. Right now! He will have your head!" She tried to yell but in a whisper.

One of his men that was already dismounted from his horse, he unsheathed his sword and put it to my mother's throat yelling at my mother. "Quiet woman! You don't talk unless you are spoken to."

My mother kept her head bowed, then I hurried to bowed my head. It was the first time I saw the king. I always heard rumors about our king. I would have never imagined he would come to our small farm. His dark presence is not welcoming.

Being lost in my head again, the king stopped in front of me. I still had my head bowed, I didn't dare move a muscle. With one word he could kill me and my family.

"The girl."

He only spoke two words, those two words he spoke was enough. One of the king's men, took my arm. It was enough strength to put me on my feet. He pushed me into the carriage. The king followed behind me. He sat on one side of the carriage and I sat on the other side. I didn't dare speak or even look at him. I am too lowly, I don't have the right to look at him; I can feel his presence.

"Return to the castle!" The king ordered his soldiers.

***

After a short little while in the carriage, the whole ride was silent. I only hear his deep breathing and the horses racing to the castle. My heart felt like it would beat out of my chest. We arrived at the castle, the castle was grand. Little did I know these stone walls would be my home.

I heard from my father that the last king was kind and generous. Nothing like the king that sits on the throne now. My mother said this king is cruel and heartless. That I was never to set foot in the capital where the castle is because of the new king and his heartless soldiers.

The towns people all kneeling in front of the new king. He became king three years ago, he fought many battles for the old king and won. It has been said the new king has stars from each battle he has won. Any man that dared to fight him, had no chance in hell to beat him. He is very skilled in battle, war, he was the king's right-hand man. The old king never had children so it would be right for the hand of the king now to take his place.

The king took my hand and pulled me out of the carriage. I could only stare at my feet, my worn out clothes and shoes don't belong in a place like this. I don't belong to a place like this.

"Bath her. I want her in my chambers."

The king pulled the wooden doors opened, and he walked into the castle. Two servants girls grabbed my arms and pulled me into the castle. We walked up and down different hallways and stairs until we finally reach the room I would be taking a bath. The two servants ripped off my old shoes and clothes. It wasn't much to rip off but I felt so uncomfortable.

I've never been naked before. I would bath in my undergarments at my parent's farm in the barn. No one has seen my naked body before. Not even Damian has seen me. My naked body is for my husband to see. I am old enough to marry now, I am at the right age to produce an heir. I have to save myself for marriage. My parents doesn't have anything to give anyone for my hand. I only have my virginity. It's the only hope for me to find a good husband. I want to give myself to my husband for the first time. I don't want to shame myself or my family.

My mind stopped wondering when the two servants scrubbed me down with lye soap. The soap started to irritate my skin and started to hurt. Maybe I can get the servants to talk to me.

"Why I'm I here?""Shhh..." "We aren't supposed to talk to you."

"Why?" I questioned the girls. Hopefully I get an answer from them. They look only a few years younger than I am. "Please tell me."

"Done."

I was pulled out of the bath and the two servants girls put me on a blue silk night undergarment. "Is there more to my dress?" "Shhh.. Go lay down on the bed." "No I will not."

"He's going to come any minute now."

The woman quietly said something under her breath, I didn't understand it before she left the room. The room was cold and dark, the only light in the room was the fireplace. My stomach growling of hunger. If only they would have came after dinner I wouldn't be so hungry. I took a blanket off the bed and wrapped it around my shoulders in front of the fireplace.

After a few minutes staring into the fire, I could feel someone's dark presence in the room with me. The king moved to me, I quickly bowed.

"Raise."

I still didn't dare look at him. I still had the blanket around my shoulders. He ripped off the blanket.

"Look at me."

The king spoke. I could feel his authority in his voice. Something about his dominant aura that made my skin crawl.

"I don't dare to... your highness." "I didn't say talk. I said look at me."

I fear he would hurt me if I didn't do want he commanded. I slowly look up at him. His dark eyes staring into my soul. The side of his face was burnt, it must have been from a battle. The scar on his face made me sad and I wonder want hardships he had to endure in battle to get so many scars. The king's scars made him look even scarier.

"Undress and get on the bed.""Why am I here? I don't belong here.""I said get undress and get on the bed." "Please let me go.""No and that is final."

He walked closer to me, I walked backwards to get away from him. I backed into a wall, he ran over to me. Grabbed my wrists pushing me into the wall.

"Please your highness let me leave. I want to go back to my family and farm.""You can never leave."

There was no emotion in his voice, only coldness. I have to get through to him, I have to beg him to let me go.

I closed my eyes with tears running down my face. "Please your highness.""I said no.""Please."

"Have you been touched by a man.""Why?""Answer the question .""I've only been kissed your highness."

I looked up at him, hopefully he can tell I'm telling the truth. He didn't say anything to me, with one arm grabbing both my wrist above my head then rubbing down below. Where I've never been touched before, I moved every way possible to get him off of me. My undergarments became wet. The sensation made me uncomfortable, I never experienced something like this before.

The king smirked and threw me in the bed. I didn't have time to react, when he ripped off his shirt. His shirt ripped into pieces, the king showing off his solid and defined muscles. With one hand he held onto my wrist and then with his other hand, he loosened his belt; removing his pants.

I screamed and screamed for someone or anyone to help me. "Help! Please your highness, you don't have to do this." "Stop screaming."

He moved his muscular body, hovering my delicate body without hesitation. He didn't care if I was screaming or crying, he was going to make me his. I would be ruined. It seems like my screaming and cries made him even more aroused.

He ripped the blue silk night undergarment into pieces. I screamed even more, cried even harder. My eyes widened, he kissed me firmly on the lips. He kissed me so hard I couldn't breathe, he was taking my oxygen away. I started to whimper, with every kiss, I never kissed him back it had him angrier with me.

"Kiss back."

He bit my lip, blood coming from my lips, he didn't care. He kept kissing me, I slowly kissed him back in fear of his wrath. I didn't want him to hurt me even more. Little did I know the night was not over for me. The king was not satisfied yet with me.

"Please your highness have mercy." He moaned, "I will not show mercy on you."

I tried moving my legs, so he would move off of me. I tried kicking and everything I could think of, I am still struggling to be set free. He forcefully moved my legs wider so he would have a better view.

"No! Please I won't be available to find a good husband." "I am all you need."

He almost tried calming me down, he careless my right check then he held my waist so tight nearly cutting off my circulation.

"No! Please stop I love someone else."

He stopped for a moment. I squirmed until he grabbed a cloth and forced it down my mouth. He grabbed my neck and began to push down on it.

"You will never love another man but me!"

He barked at me. I never seen him so angry in so little time. Was it something I said or something I did?

I stopped fighting, I didn't have any fight in me left. He won, if I moved I would be dead; we both knew it. He pressed down on my neck more than kissed me. I blacked out.

***   I opened my eyes, I don't remember what happened to me after I blacked out. I quickly blinked my eyes and noticed someone sitting down in a chair in the room. The person's face in the darkness, with the light of the fireplace. It was hard to see anything. I sat up on the bed, "You are mine now."

"What?"

I moved the blanket off of me, a blood stains where on the bed, and I was completely naked. I tried covering myself with the blanket.

"I'm done with you for the night. Just remember I only went easy on you."

I remember everything happened till I blacked out. From the blood stains and the soreness I feel down below in my lady parts. The king put on his clothes and slammed the door behind him leaving me in this cold dark room alone.

The king raped me; the king did despicable things to me. I have to escape from here, I don't belong here. Damian will never marry me but I always have my family. I have to escape…

Chapter 2
By His Darkness

I quickly got out of the bed, my lady parts are still sore from what he did to me. My dress was on the floor ripped, I grabbed my dress and put it dress on. I don't have anything else to wear and I don't have anything to fix the dress. At my family's farm I can fix my dress. This dress has lasted me three years I've had to sew it up a few times, but buying a new dress would feed all the animals for a month and probably have money left over. I can't get away from here with nothing on. I have to leave here, I don't want to be part of the king's harem. You never see the woman again after they enter the castle. From what the king did to me that might be his plan for me. He might want me to join his harem and have sex with random men. The only man that I want to have sex with is Damian. Even now I'm not sure if Damian would still want me. I am a ruined woman now.

I can't think of that right now, I have to escape from the hell. I have to think of a way out of here. If I don't leave this place I will be enslaved and I have to surrender all to his or the harems, sexual desires.

I walked over to the door and opened the door. Two knights with swords standing on each side of the door.

"Miss we have strict orders to not let you leave your room. Please go back inside."

I nodded and close my door. There's no way I can talk them into letting me leave. I walked around the room and I ran over to the window. I am on the fourth floor of the castle. If I would jump down I could break something and I wouldn't be able to run away. If I do break something I could get an infection and died. I don't plan on doing that any time soon. If I'm here any longer, that might be a choice.

I can't jump out of the window, but what can I do.

I thought to myself pacing back and forth in my room. My candle that's lit in my room is flickering, the wax is melted enough that the candle is about to go out. I still can see because of the fireplace, but the candle is about to go out. The candle.

I can use the candle to escape!

I thought to myself, I looked around the room and the red curtains beside the window I can use. I can lit the curtains on fire with the candle. That might just work it can distract the guards enough so I can get out of the room then out of this place.

I lit the curtains with the candle, then put the candle beside the wooden storage box on the floor. When the knights come in and see the flame the will think the candle just by the flame caught on fire by itself.

I screamed and the two knights come rushing in. The two knights were busy with trying to put out the flame when I ran out of the room.

My plan worked, I am finally going to be free!

I walked down the same hallway that come in. Another two knights walking towards me.

"Help fire!"

The knights ran passed me and my heart pounding out of my chest. This is not going to be good if I get caught. I ran down the stairs, then when I got to the hallway that lead to the front of the castle's doors. I stopped there was another set of knights with swords guarding the doors.

What am I going to do.

I just stood there peeking my head around the corner to see the knights. A man presented was behind me he touched my shoulder.

The king! He found me!

I jumped and the man covered my face with his hands so I wouldn't scream. "Shhh... I'm here to help."

All I could do was to look at him. I looked at him confused, he has knights armor on. Why would he help me?

"I know what the king did to you. I am disgusted by his actions. I want to help! You don't have much time."

I nodded and He released his hand away from my mouth. He walked past me then yelled for the two knights guarding the door.

"Go help the men upstairs, I'll guard the door."

The two knights ran up the stairs taking the servants stairs. The servant stairs were on the left side of the door. I ran past the man that help me. I ran and ran as fast as my legs would go. I held onto my dress that was ripped and kept on running until I saw my family's farm. My legs made me stop, I took a second to catch my breath, then ran again to my house. My house was nothing special one room house with everyone sleeping on the floors. The house was always dirty and falling apart. My father did want he could with it and still took care of the animals. My mother grows a vegetable garden it was enough to feed our family.

I ran inside and opened the door.

***Victor POV

"I want our nations to make a treaty. Both our kingdoms need this.""Yours more than mine.""Yes that is true."

My beautiful woman is lying in the bed I left her. I want her, I need her. Now I have her I'll never let her go. Maybe it was wrong of me to do what I did. I went to check on her and I saw her with that other man my anger got the best of me. She was laying on a blanket in the wheat fields and I wanted to go up to her but another man came up to her first. They looked like they love each other. Just thinking of them together makes my blood boil. She belongs to me. I am king. Ivy, I love her so much, I waited long enough to come back to her, but she doesn't remember me. I need to show her, but I have to hurry up and make this treaty with King Leo.

With his great army right now he could take over this kingdom. I will not give him the satisfaction of taking my kingdom away from me. The kingdom just won the last battle two years ago just before the old king died. Just before I became king, my lands can not take another battle. In a few years my lands would be healed, but I need to protect my kingdom. I would lay down my life for my kingdom.

"Is there anything that might persuade you in signing this treaty? My kingdom has many beautiful young women, and you can have any woman in my harem..."

I was cut off when one of my guards banging on the door. "Come in!"

The guard that was banging on my door was my most trusted guard. He's my younger brother and I trust him with my life. He already knows about her and what happened after I got back from the last battle. The old king sent us both in front lines.

"Your highness. There's been a fire and the girl escaped.""What girl?!""She did."

I ran out of my room breaking everything that was in the hallway. I finally got her and she escaped? How did she escape? I have to find her if it's the last thing I do.

***Ivy's POV

I ran inside and opened the door. Everyone was sound asleep on the floor. When my father heard the door open he quickly got up and grabbed his sword and pointed at me.

"You?""Father!"

My father saw that it was me that came through the door, he lowered his sword. My mother and siblings heard the commotion and woke up from their beds.

"The king!""What? Why are you here?""The king did... he did..." Speak up woman."

"He did... despicable means to me.""What?""Yes."

"You whore! You spread your legs like a whore!""Scandal! Who would marry you now?"

My mother slapped me across the face. "I had high hopes you would marry off well. You are not my daughter anymore. I'm ashamed of you. You have shamed us all. You are no longer welcome here."

My mother's words felt like thousands of swords cutting into my heart. I was raped by the king and my family is ashamed of me. They don't see me as their daughter anymore. I have no place to go.

"Please I can't go back to the castle!""Scandal!"

My eyes watered, I tried pulling on my mother's hem of dress. "Mom... Please."

On my knees begging my mother to look at me, to say something. I looked over to my father, he didn't even want to look at me. I shamed both of them. I am the victim.

"I'm the victim!"

A hard slap came from my father, the slap made me fall back a little; then he pulled my hair roughly to stand up on my feet with a stare of rage and disgust. After my father let go of my hair, I held my face in one hand. The red hand print emerged on my face is stinging. Tears falling from my eyes.

I already knew the truth, but I didn't want it to be true. I shamed myself and them, what my mother said was right; they did have high hopes I would marry off well.

"Get out!" He yelled, the first time I heard my father yell. He has always been a soft-spoken man, never raise his voice about anything until now.

I could feel his cold and dark presence behind me. The king standing behind me with a smirk. "She can work for me."

"I don't want to hear anything that becomes of her." My father nodded and my mother sitting down crying.

The king's guard pulled me away from my family. I tried to fight back, but with one swoop, the king's guard puts me on the king's horse. We rode into the darkness. Only the night stars to guide us to the castle. The king holding my waist with one hand, then holding the rope around the horn of the saddle to keep us on the horse and for me not to go anywhere.

"I wouldn't be worried about them. They are already dead to you ." "You wouldn't hurt them, would you?" He didn't say anything, he just held onto my waist tighter.

Now I would be his. I was swollen by his darkness and I have no way of escaping. He got want he wanted. My family was my only hope. For a moment I thought my family would take me back, but I have shamed them. I was lost to them, my parents do not have a daughter anymore.

"Ivy! Ivy! Let her go!"

I looked back and my Damian was riding a horse to catch up to us. I wiggle out of the king's grip, it made the king and his guards stop. Damian got off his horse, then ran to me and hugged me. I hugged him back.

"Release her or you're dead!""Your highness I am here to pay for her. I can sell you any horses or money to pay for her."

I whispered, "What are you doing? You don't have to do this. We can still run."

The king ordered his guards to lower their swords. They were ready to kill us both with one order from the king.

"Please your highness. We want to marry.""Never!"

The king pulled out his sword and with one hit, the king slid Damian's throat.

"No!"

Damian in a pool of his own blood. I went on my knees and pulled Damian's body close to mine. Blood still coming from his neck, his breathing became slower and slower. The king killed the only man I have ever loved.

"No!"

I cried and cried, the king walked over to us. The king kicked away Damian's cold, dead body.

"Now you are mine. You don't have anyone."

The king walked to his horse and got on then nodded his head to his guards. Just like before with one swoop, the king's guard puts me on the king's horse. We rode the rest of the castle in darkness. I cried the whole way to the castle. I must have passed out, I woke up in my room I was in before.

Chapter 3
Monster

Victor's POV

Now she only has me. She has no one. No one deserves this beautiful goddess. Not even me, but I am the only one that will have her. She will be forever mine. I lost her once I will not do that again. She means too much to me. Now I have everything I ever wanted. I have her. All that I need is here beautiful, sweet Ivy. She's mine forever.

***Ivy's POV

I must have passed out, I woke up in my room I was in before, because the king is sitting on a chair in the room. With only the light of the fireplace in the room. The king gripping the hands of the chair, then sit up after he noticed I am awake.

"You're finally awake?"

I didn't nod or say anything; this man, this king killed the only man I have ever loved. Even my own parents doesn't want me. I have no one. This man in front of me ruin my life. He ruined my life... I have to get away from this monster. He's not a man; he's a monster.

"Why did you run away from this castle?" "To tell the truth your highness. To get away from you."

"From me?"

The king slowly got up from his chair, slowly making his way to the bed. He slowly came on the bed and I just stared at him watching his every move. He came closer to me only a few inches more we would be kissing.

"You know better than to run away from me, don't you?" "Just kill me!" The king chuckled "Don't tempt me princess. What's with the yelling?"

With tears falling and my fists into balls, "You killed him! He was going to pay you..for me." "It wasn't enough. You belong to me." "I don't belong to anyone."

He grabbed my face and pulled me closer to his mouth. "You belong to your king."

I pushed away from and got up from the bed. "You are no king of mine."

He spoke, but I didn't hear a thing that came out of his mouth. My mind wandered around the room figuring out how to kill the beast. Kill this monster.

The king had a small dagger on his belt. I can use his own dagger on him. How can I kill someone? But this man killed my love of my life. The only man I have ever loved. He single-handedly ruined my life. I have to make him pay.

I ran to the chair that had his belt draped on top of it. He must have taken it off when I was asleep. He had his belt on when we were riding on his horse. When we were on his horse, his belt was rubbing against my back.

I started slowly walking closer to the door. "You stay away from me. I will take this dagger and I will leave."

"You will not leave this castle or leave this room." The king started to climb off of the bed. "You are mine!"

"Monster...you stay away from me!"

I pointed the dagger at the king. "Stay away from me. I will kill you if you don't stay away from me... or I'll kill myself." I closed my eyes and put the dagger against my throat.

Without a thought the king got on his feet, and He laughed, catching me by my wrist with his spare hand and spinning me around, so my back was to him and the dagger is still in my hands, but at my throat. My pulse racing, his arm moving her body closer to his.

"Drop the dagger. I don't want to see blood on this beautiful body of yours." He whispered huskily against her ear, pressing his pelvis into the small of her back. "Do you want me inside you again? Do you want your womb to be filled with my seed?"

Moving his free hand up and down the side of my body. To stop him, I dropped the dagger. He released me; I turned around and back away to create distance between us. "Stay away from me!"

"I want you."

I recoiled away from the king. The king walking towards me. Walking back trying to make distance, I tripped over a carpet and backed against the wall. I wanted to recoil further when he pushed me against the wall and clutched my wrist forcefully and pushed me against the wall again. The king blocked my way out with his body.

I think the king did it twice to scare me. My breath raced, because I am terrified of his angrier and the other way was he was standing too close to me. He killed my beloved without a thought. This man is a cold-hearted monster. I don't want to be anywhere near the heartless king.

"Get away from me!""You belong to me. I don't want any form of resistance coming from you. I have been gentle with you, but you try to escape again or do anything to anger me. You don't understand what I could do to you... My little dove.""Dove?" I whispered to myself.

The king held me close to him. "One day soon.""Soon?" "You will be my wife, my queen."

The king held my face between his fingers and squeeze my cheeks together, making them hurt; my lips are pushed together. "Soon." The king lightly kissed my lips, then walked out of my room. I stood there rubbing my cheeks. The way he held my face made my cheeks and jaw hurt.

~~~~~~~~~~~~~~~~~~~~~~~~~~~~~~~

Hey, sorry you guys! I know it's short but I'm in the middle of moving!

Chapter 4
Do You Remember: Part 1

Ivy's POV

After the king walked out of my room, I laid down on the bed. I couldn't sleep, too many thoughts of my parents, Damian and the king. What did the king meant by I would be his wife and queen? And soon?

After a few hours went by I finally found myself asleep then I woke up in a cold sweat, searching frantically around the small room. As if he "the king" were really here, his piercing charcoal gray eyes haunt my dreams, and his face, there's something about his face. The side of his face was burnt, but also familiar. I have seen him before. Long ago, but he wasn't the king, just a soldier for the old king. I know about three years ago I think around the same time the old king died. I met a man that I helped him recover from battle. It could be him.... Could? He didn't have burn marks on his face.

That man never said anything to me when he was recovering in my family's barn. He was hesitant for someone or anyone to help him. I made him comfortable enough with me to help him. I changed his bandages and fed him. At first the man wouldn't eat anything, but he was just thirsty. I don't remember what happened after that. It was so long ago I almost forgot. There's something about the king that reminds me of him. Could he be that man?

Victor's POV

Ivy still after all these years like honey, the sweetest and purest. I want her for himself; I am king, it comes with the title of King to be selfish. I want sweetest and purest Ivy to be my wife, my country's queen. I want her to be beside me and rule this country. I have high hopes for my country. My country needs a great ruler, I can't be until she's by my side. Together we can rule this country for the better.

The old king ruined this country. For three years I tried to bring this country back to glory. The old king's greediness ruined this country. My only greediness wants her. I just want her. With Ivy's pure heart, with her beside me I can do anything. We can rule this country together and bring it back to its glory. I have lived in this country my whole life and I have almost died for this country more than once. Under the old king's rule. There's nothing I wouldn't do to help my country.

Ivy's POV

It's been hours since a few female slaves came inside my room to check on me. When they came inside the room and told me about what the king wanted. I have yelled, screamed and throw anything I could get my hands on. The female slaves ran out of the room and hasn't returned since. The slaves are from neighboring countries.

They are sold for gold, land and more. Would I end up like them? Sold to another country if I don't become his?

Maybe I can borrow a slaves clothes and escape from this place. My family doesn't want me, and I am no good for them now. I can't get a husband even if I wanted to. I am ruined. With Damian gone, I have nothing holding me back here. I can leave here and start a new somewhere else. The king said he wants to be his wife, his queen. I don't want to be a queen or his wife. I want a normal life, I want a family. Now I can never have one, I'll be an old maid until I died or I could be a whore on the streets.

Leading against the window and looking outside. The doors to my room opened wide and the king barged into the room.

"Why do you insist on defying my orders?""What orders?""Don't play stupid with me. I sent up your maids to have you dressed, bathe and come stairs before this time.""You mean female slaves."

"Watch your mouth before I do something about it." I rolled my eyes and crossed my arms to my chest.

The king opened the doors again, "Come in and bathe her, dress her. I want her down stairs in the dining hall in half an hour. You have kept our guest waiting long enough."

The two female slaves walking into my room frightened, holding a dress in their arms. "Yes, your highness."

"Make sure she is dressed, and ready or it will be your heads."

The female slaves started to undressed me, when the king walked out. One of the slaves, "Please miss I do want he says. I don't want to get into trouble again." I could tell she was scared of him and what he might do, and the other slave was just as scared.

I nodded, after a few short minutes. I let them bathe and dress me. One of the girls branded my hair while the other one helped me put on the dress; she was carrying earlier. I have never seen this type of blue dye before.

"I do love this color blue.""It's the king's favorite color Miss.""We spent days before you arrived here dying your dresses different shades of blue and the colors his highness loves."

"How did you dye this shade of blue?" I expected every inch of the dress. The dress is a perfect fit for me. It does show a little too much on the breast area.

"You took different plants and berries dye them." The female slave smiled, she looked very pleased with her work and how I was admiring the shade.

The other slaved finished the last part of my brand, "I'm done, Miss you must hurry to the dining hall. It's been almost the time he said."

"Thank you, what are your names?""Beth and Gail.""Pretty names.""Miss you better hurry. Please miss."

***   I opened the doors to my room and the two guards standing outside my room. Followed me to the dining hall, quickly got up from his chair and marched over to where I was standing. He forcibly took my arm walking back over to his chair. I looked around the room, he noticed that I noticed the girls in the harems filing sexual desires and drinking ale with men. Knights and the prettier girls in the harems are around looks like another King.

The king pulling my arms closer to him, "No one will touch you. No one dare to cross me. Liquor help courage men to do what they otherwise would not. But I am king. No one dares to define me."

I rolled my eyes at the so called "King." He sat down on his chair, "Love, come sit." He pats the stool next to him and I lower my head and walked over to him. I sit next to him, and he's quick to place his rough hand on my thigh, causing me to glance up at him, "Drink and eat."

The peasants' main food was a dark bread made out of rye grain. Normally peasants ate a kind of stew called pottage made from peas, beans and onions that people normally around here have grown in their gardens. Our only sweet food was the berries, nuts and honey that they collected from the woods. The food here looks amazing and nothing I would have at my family's farm. The people here are drinking something different from what I have seen before. Normally around the village people were drinking ale, mead or cider.

The king noticed I was looking at what type of liquid the people here are drinking when he said, "We have different types of wines here. Here drink." Pushing a cup to me, "You'll like it."

I took a sip of whatever that was in the cup the king gave me. I coughed and made a twisted face at the taste. The taste was bitter, and a hint of sweetness. At the farm I would always use to drinking ale or milk, the water was always dirty and for the plants, vegetables and animals.

The king spoke up, "It's good after you get past the taste."

I nodded and took another sip of the wine he gave me. I can feel my face is flush, and my body seemed to be more relaxed.

"Do you want more wine?"

I'm sure I am feeling the effects of the wine. I turned my gazed down to the half-empty cup. My breathing was altered, my flesh was blushes pink from the wine and starting to be aroused.

I looked up from my cup to see the other king staring at me. The king sitting next to me gripped the hem of my dress noticed also.

"Are you enjoying the night?" "Yes I am." With a curious look on his face, he smirked. "I would have a better night if I could use her tonight."

"King Leo you can't have any women in my harem." The king opened his arms to the crowd and took a sip of his wine, "But beside this one, she is to be my wife and queen." "Oh, my apologies King Victor."

***

So the king that was seated next to me is named, King Victor. King Victor couldn't keep his eyes off of me the whole dinner service. The knights that helped me escape the first day he's standing up straight, protecting the king.

Chapter 5
Do you Remember: Part 2

✱ **Victor's POV

With my Ivy in the room the other women in the room didn't hold a candle to her, and they seemed to know it although it didn't stop them from trying to compete with my attention. Not one of them appealed to me as much as Ivy; they didn't have her beauty, innocent, or gentle nature.

Vance's POV

Seeing Ivy in her blue gown was something to see. When we first met I only had a glimpse of her beauty because the wall was very dark. Only light was from the candles in the hallways and the stars outside the windows. I can see why Victor care for her. I understand why he cares for her, Victor has told me everything.

The battle was over, he was coming back to the castle. I was still with my unit, he went ahead of everyone else. Victor was the old king's right-hand man. Now I am the Victor's right hand man. Victor said he was hurt very badly, he almost died coming back to the castle.

The king was sick, so he needed to go back a heads of everyone else. It didn't matter if Victor was hurt or not. He needed to be with the king.

Victor said he was almost to the castle when he found a barn and stopped to rest. Badly bruised, almost didn't make it. That is when Ivy found him in her family's barn. For the next couple of days Ivy took care of him, she nursed him back to health. She was sweet and gentle with him, no one has ever been that way with him. Not even our mother she didn't even know our mother only relatives.

He said that her family didn't know about her caring for him. She said her father would put him out of his misery. He would possibly kill her too for helping someone. She did it anyways and help cared for him. She did her chores then snuck into the barn and redid his new bandages, gave him food, drink. What little she did get she would give it to him. He didn't know about it till much later he told me.

After becoming king, and remembering what she did for him. He checked in on her, and he saw her with another man his blood boiled, and he decided that it's now or never, she will be his.

I know his reason for being her here to the castle but as once a knight himself, I don't understand why Victor took away her innocent.

***Ivy's POV

After dinner was over, the king wanted me to join him outside to look up at the stars. I declined his offer and told him I wasn't feeling good. I told him that all the wine got to my head and I'm going to lie down.

The two guards, from earlier escorted me back to my room. When I noticed from the corner of my eye that the King that asked about me, as if I was a part of the harem and not as the king soon to be bride. The king Leo talking to one of the guards in the hallway.

The king look old enough to be my father. Middle-aged man with blonde hair and hazel eyes. Even his beard matched his hair color. He does have some white and black hair mixed with his blond hair. For a king his hair is messy but taken care of. I guess I had too much to drink at dinner. A lot stronger than what I am use too.

My head is spinning and I slowly walked to my bed and laid down on top. The doors open and the king walks in.

"I told you I didn't want to see the stars.""I wanted to check on you."

I sat up on top of the bed, the king sat on the corner of my bed. "Come here." He pulled me closer to him, he put my head down on top of his lap. My head rest on his lap, and then he began to run his fingers through my hair.

I tried moving away from him but he pulled me back, and doing the same thing with his fingers again. At least what he's doing with my hair feels good. I don't even remember my mother doing this to my hair.

Victor's POV

I ran my fingers through her beautiful hair. She is so beautiful when she's in my arms. I'll never let her go. I'll never let anything happen to her.

"Do you remember...who I am?""I think you're the man I nursed back to health. A few years ago.""Yes I am.""But why?"

She cupped her hand with my face and rubbed her fingers on top of my scars on my face. "I don't remember you have scars on your face."

"I didn't have them till I came back to the castle. No one told you what happen the night that I became king?""No."

I ran my fingers through her again, and I was about to tell her what happened. She started to snore, I smiled at her. I can tell her what happened that night another time. She just needs to sleep the wine off.

Chapter 6

Wolves Part 1

Victor POV

She even beautiful when she sleeps. I could stare at her all night, but I have a business to attend too. If I don't, then my country might be looking at another war.

As slowly and softly as I could I moved Ivy's head off my lap and onto a pillow. She moved around a little but didn't wake up. She is still snoring and still looking beautiful as ever.

I quietly moved away from the bed and opened the doors to her room, walked out. My guards followed me, and told my brother to inform everyone we are going to have a meeting. Everyone must attend.

***

After a short few minutes all of my knights were either sitting around my around the table or standing. My brother at my right hand, the ones sitting down at the table are the knights I've known for years that I trust.

"As everyone knows in a week the kingdom is to have a festival. I want this to go as smoothly as possible.""Yes your highness."

Everyone in the agreed that everyone would try to make this festival go as smoothly as possible. I want King Leo to have a memorable time here in my kingdom. I want him to agree to be allies, then we could grow our kingdoms. My country would be less likely to be in another war if we are allies with King Leo. Maybe one day we can have our kingdoms united. Then we would be unstoppable.

***Ivy's POV

I flicker my eyes then I opened them then I noticed King Victor is not still in my room. Where he was sitting on the cold, he must have left the room when I fell asleep. A part of me is glad he didn't do anything when I fell asleep from the alcohol in my system.

Speaking of alcohol, I stood up from my bed and walked over to the table that has some bread and cheese, and more wine. When I stood up, I don't feel the effects of the alcohol anymore. Plus the castle is oddly dark and quiet right now.

I walked over to my doors, normally I have two guards, guarding my door, because King Victor doesn't want me to escape again. Just the thought of him, I rolled my eyes, of course with every chance I get I'm going to try to run away from hell. I want to find another kingdom where I can make a new start.

I slowly opened one of the doors, nothing. Nothing happened, no yelling to get back to my room or no swords pointed at me. Even the swords a cross in front of me, a few times now they have done that and the sound from the swords, that's what scared me to jump back. But nothing, I pointed my head out of the door. There were no guards, guarding my door.

I have no idea why, maybe King Victor feels like he can trust me, or he has called them to do something. I don't know why there aren't posted at my door, but I'm going to use this change and try to escape.

I grabbed a blanket off the bed and grabbed the food off the table. I drank the wine and tied the surrounding blanket. The food can last me a couple of days if I make it last. I have done with much less than this many of times. That's not a problem for me, my problem is the dress that I had to put on. Would make me stick out and I would be noticed and forced to come back here.

The idea that I had earlier, I could borrow a slaves clothes and escape from this place. The slaves clothes are not royal colors, so I wouldn't be noticed as much as I would in this dress.

I ran across the hall into my slaves room, luckily they were also not in their rooms. One of the slaves would possibly if they saw me would get the attention of a knight or worse the king. To win favors, and they could ask for anything that their heart desires. Even possibly they could ask not to be a slave anymore.

I grabbed an outfit and ran back into my room to grab my blanket bag I made for myself. The darkness of the castle will help in my escape. I walked in the shadows of the darkness to not be seen by anyone. I made my way to the front doors. No one was guarding the front doors, I can't believe it. There must be something big going on. I wonder what it must be.

I can't think of that now and I have to leave this place. I grabbed the handle of the door and pushed the door open. It took all of my strength, the door is heavy really heavy. I cannot open the door by myself. But I have to try, I can't give up. I pushed it again and this time it wasn't hard to open it. Someone helped me opened it, I looked over and it was a woman from the harems that tried to get King Victor's attention earlier.

"You?""Go go! Before they come back!"

I nodded and said thank you, and I ran for it. I still ran into the darkness of the woods. Someone in the village would definitely remember me from when I was brought here for the first time or anytime. The dark woods would be my best chance. I ran into the woods hoping the knights on top of the castle, didn't see him. They watch over the castle, I am not that lucky the knights on top of the castle did see me. They yelled for more knights. The kingdom is aware that I am trying to escape.

Distance was all that mattered. I am not going to stop for anything. I ran and ran as fast as my feet could take me. Even when I slid down, hurt my knees and blood coming down. I'm not going to stop, I have to make it to another country.

My lugs couldn't take it anymore. I ran as fast as I could. Every bone and mussel hurt, my mind kept saying, "Go! Go!", but my body couldn't. I did stop, I am so close to the edge of our country and I'll be out of this kingdom for good.

Chapter 7

Wolves Part 2

Taking to catch my breath, I can't see anything everything is pitch black but the stars in the sky. About to start running again when I can hear growling and snarling behind me. I quickly turned around, and saw a pair of wolves eyes staring at me. Many color eyes some are amber and brown or even gold.

I knew it meant danger if I stay where I am at. I turned around and ran for the wall that boards out two countries. If only I can get over the wall or the gate I can be free of this kingdom.

I have to find a way around the wall or climb up a large tree to get over the wall. Normally people would have to have a permission to leave the country. In order to get permission, you would need the king or his court.

The walls have torches that's lit, I turned around it was definitely seen a pack of wolves running after me. I turned around and put my back against the wall.

One wolf began to howl and the rest of them all stop, drawn to join in like they have been invited to a family feast. My father once said wolves claws are sharp enough to be useful when taking down prey or digging a den for the pups. Those claws on the wolves could rip me apart.

Vance's POV

My brother sent all of his men to find Ivy again. Riding my horse into the woods, the knights on top of the castle said she was going to this way. My guess if I were her, I would head for the wall and make a break for it.

With a few of my men beside me, everyone stopped riding their horse when we heard the howling of wolves. The wolves in the woods around here are beautiful but deadly. The wolves around here are known to kill livestock and small animals. I'm sure they would surely eat her.

I quickly realized the girl could be in serious trouble because of the howling of the wolves. I quickened my pace on my horse, then coming where Ivy and the wolves are. I quickly got off my horse and I pulled out my sword from its scabbard in one smooth, well-practiced motion. Getting between Ivy and the wolves.

The other wolves backed away. Then it looked like the alpha male coming towards me. I pointed my sword to the alpha male, and we made eye contact. He knows I'm not backing down. The alpha wolf narrowed his glaze, I followed my sword to where he was looking at.

Ivy held onto my shirt, I didn't break eye contact the alpha wolf. The alpha wolf made some type of howl, then walked away. The other wolves backed away then followed their pack leader.

Once I didn't see the wolves anymore, I put down my sword then turned to Ivy. "Trying to escape again are we?"

She just looked at me, "I'm not going back." She tried to make a run for it. I pushed her back to the wall.

"You are coming with me. The king wants you.""I am not going back."

"Yes you are." I forcibly grabbed her and put her on top of my horse, then tied her hands to my horse. I made sure that the ropes wasn't too tight to cut off circulation but tight enough where she wouldn't escape. Then I jumped on my horse then began to ride back to the castle.

"You are just like him! Please let me go! He doesn't have to know we saw each other!""I'm just following orders Princess. He's my brother.""Don't call me that! Brother?"

Chapter 8
If I Were King

Ivy's POV

Brothers? Did he just say, they are brothers? Some facial expressions are the same, but they look completely different. The king looks a few years older, and he does look younger. Why did he call me princess? That sounded more like an insult than a complement.

I kicked and kicked to get free, he tightened his grip on my waist, he's just like his brother. If he wasn't he would let me go already or help me escape. He did once, why is now any different?

"You let me go once, why is now any different?"

He did say anything, I caught him off guard. I don't think he was thinking I was going to ask that. But it's true? Why is now any different. This time I'm even close escape then I did last time. I could hurt him right now since he is off guard.

His grip loosened just enough where I could wiggle off the horse. He slowed down his horse, I wiggle right off the horse. He's really is letting me go?

"You're letting me go?" "Yes." "Why?" "Don't worry about that for now. Go and don't come back. Get as far away as possible." "Thank you."

I started running in the directions I was going before. I heard him call out to me, "Remember, you do need permission to be in another kingdoms land...."

I ran to fast and I didn't hear the last part of his sentence. I was for sure not going to turn back around and ask him what he said.

Vance POV

It was tough for me to let her go. I could've got praised by my brother and my people, since she's going to be our queen. Even gold coins from him or even both. She doesn't need to be here, if she doesn't want too. I'm not anything like Victor, I know when a woman doesn't want to lay in bed with me. Even I do wish I had Ivy in my bed chambers. She has grown on me, but I hope she gets as far away as possible and never returns here. Nothing good can become of it of her returning.

Knowing my brother, he's not going to take it lightly that she ran. He's going to send out even more men to search for her and bring her back. Even to search for her in other kingdoms. I hope she doesn't get found out. Hopefully she has some wits about her. Not going into an enemy's land. She can end up dead. I do wish the best for her.

If she does come back, I want to try to win her affections and steal her away from Victor. How Victor treats her, it will be easy. I could even ask for her hand since I'm not married, and he's been bugging me about marriage. Ivy can be mine, and everything else can follow.

Victor might be right I need a good woman on my side. Then I can get what I really want.

I smirked to myself while riding back to the castle. After I noticed I had gone closer to the castle, I picked up my pace of my horse. So that it would look like I was racing back to the castle, Victor standing in front of the castle doors pacing back and forth. I jumped down from my horse, Victor running to me, "Did you find her? Is she hurt?"

"I did see her, but she cross over the wall on the east wall. I had to come back." "Why didn't you stop her?" "I couldn't." "Oh right."

Victor remembered there's a treaty that says, anyone that wants to be in another kingdom needs permission from a king or queen. If they do not have a king's permission then it's up to the king's decision if he wants death, or another slave. If it's a man, then the kings might recruit the man to be a soldier in his army.

If I were king, I would have anyone who went over my walls to be a part of my army. They escaped their land for a reason and knew what was going to happen. Then I would have the strongest army. The woman that should cross over would be sears slaves. My harems would be huge. Other Kings would love my harem, then would want to be allies with me to enjoy my harem. They would HAVE to because I would have a great army of soldiers. That would only happened if I were king but Victor is king.

Ivy's POV

When I climbed up that tree then went over the wall, thank goodness I fell into a haystack. It did hurt my arm and ass when I fell down.

I stood up and ran into the green barn that was close. I didn't want anyone in the house to notice me.

   I noticed when I went into the barn everything is green. The inside and outside the barn and stalls for the animals are all green. Even the hand tools rack, pitchfork, shovel all were green. Someone must love the color green or this kingdoms color is green. Maybe they have a law that everything has to be green.

   Looking at my clothes, what I'm going to do. I am wearing nothing green. Green doesn't look good on me. If I am here I have to wear it, even if I don't like wearing the color. If someone saw me, I could get reported to this land's king. He could be even more messed up in the head then Victor. I have to find something to wear. I heard my father talking about a kingdom that wears all green, but I didn't hear the rest of what he was saying because I had to hurry up and do my chores.

Chapter 9
Coffee

Ivy's POV

This kingdom must be the kingdom that wears all green. Walking around in the barn, I looked to my right and I can see outside the window a farmer's wife is hanging out clothes to dry on a clothesline. I know at my family's farm, my mother picked the sunniest pot on the farm. She would hand wash each of them clothes, with soap she made herself. She would make me shake out the clothes first then use a wooden clothes spin and hang them on the clothesline. After a few hours the clothes would be done, then I would have to take down the clothes then take them inside. All while my father was taking care of the animals or corn, replanting something. From looking at the farmer's wife, what I did at the farm.

After a few minutes, the farmer's wife walked into the house. I don't even stop to think, I ran to the clothesline and picked the clothes that would fit me. I grabbed the clothes then, I ran into the woods for cover. The farm or farmer's wife didn't see me, if they did they would've ran outside and chase me. I took a deep sigh of relief, and looked behind me further down into the woods. A few feet from me, a huge tree was standing. Perfect for hiding behind while changing into my new clothes.

Now I can go into any part of this kingdom and not be noticed. I put the clothes on that I stole from the farmer's wife, and folded my clothes that I'm not wearing. But I don't like steal, this is my first time sealing something. I do feel awful, but I will remember this and I will repay them somehow, someday I will.

The green shirt is twice the size that I normally wear. I rip the bottom of the shirt, then wrap the edges of the shirt around my waist, so the shirt would fit me. The rest of the shirt that I ripped off, I put it down on the branch of the tree. So it wouldn't get dirty on the ground.

After putting on my skirt, the skirt is long enough where it covers my shoes. I didn't want to steal shoes too, and make it twice as worse. It was already bad enough that I stole clothes and shoes too. One, that would raise suspicions. Clothes can fly off of the clothesline all the time. Second, my debt to them would be even more.

I took the rest of the ripped shirt and layout the folded clothes I was wearing before, laid them on ripped shirt. I tied the edges of the ripped shirt into a knot. My mother showed me how to do this before, she made a bag out of ripped old clothes, rags. Then she would carry it around when she plants the seeds. It did what it was supposed to do, to be a bag and it worked. This will have to work too. I want to keep my clothes because if I need it then I can use it. Maybe if I need to sell my clothes, then I will.

I have to survive out here somehow, someway. I don't even know anyone outside my kingdom. My kingdom is in the past. I don't know if this kingdom will be my home or I'll keep going and find somewhere I can call home. I do know I have to keep moving.

I walked out of the woods, onto a dirt path. I followed the dirt path till I got to a small village. People were smiling and laughing. Everyone seemed to have a great time. Children playing, people trying to sell things fruits, vegetables and handmade goods. Some of the item would look beautiful in a home. In the life I should've had with Damian.

I was walking through the village, when I look around at these beautiful women in front of me, chatting and talking to their lovers. My heart hurts because I can never have that now. They don't know how lucky they are.

I kept walking through the village until I found another dirt path. I walked and walked, until I noticed a two girls walking in the same distraction as me. They were armed to arm, laughing and giggling to each other. They sort of look like sisters, both of their hair looked long brown in braids down their backs. Both of them are wearing the same shade of green.

Victor's POV

Today is the first day of the festival and Ivy is missing. I wanted this festival to be filled with laughter and joy. Now I want to cancel the whole thing. My beautiful Ivy isn't here with me to enjoy it with. I have plenty of women in my harem. But I don't want any of them. I want Ivy, I want to bring her back. I have to send out my men and bring her back! At the end of this festival, my people will have a wedding to celebrate.

"We have to find her! Bring her back!""Should we send out men to find her?""Yes, I'm sure she's in one of the surrounding kingdoms." "Should we cancel the festival?""No! No! It must go on.""I will send out troops to all the surrounding kingdoms on your order, sir.""Yes."

My trusted and loyal brother, I know I can trust him to bring her back. Out of all my men or my kingdom, I trust Vance. We have fought many battles, I remember them all. Vance was by my side the whole time. We look after each other, we were battle buddies. To return the gratitude for Vance being beside me in battle and protect me now I want to show my thanks and I want to have my blessings for a wife. I want him to be just as happy as I am with Ivy. Maybe our sons will fight together in battle too.

Ivy's POV

I followed the girls to a large tree in the middle of a field. A large tree with green apples hanging down. A few villages filling up baskets. No one is paying anyone, people are eating the apples right off the tree. Everyone is happy and enjoying the apples and everyone's company.

I put my arms around my stomach when I heard my stomach growling. The two women in front of me turned back to me, "You must be new. Come and eat."

I nodded, one of the women ran up the tree playfully and pulled a branch down, she looked like she was holding it down. The other woman walked over pulled a green apple off the tree. She tossed the apple to me, I didn't realize what she was going to do when I almost dropped the apple. But I managed to catch it.

I looked down to rub the green apple on my shirt and when I looked up, I noticed the two women doing the same thing again. But the woman is tossing the apples on the ground. I took a big bite of the apple, I kept on eating and eating the apple. The apple was so delicious, it tasted like what I imagine what heaven would be like. I've always had red apples and that was rare, but never tasted anything like this before.

"These green apples are only grow here in this kingdom.""They are so good."

"Here have another one." She tossed me another apple. I caught it, "Thank you."

"Where are you from?""The kingdom next door."

I looked down, my kingdom is the only kingdom that borders this kingdom. The other side of this kingdom is water.

"We won't tell anyone."

The woman understood, or they have met someone like me before. Both women nodded their heads after the oldest out of the two said they wouldn't tell anyone.

"I like your green dresses.""Thank you, I sew them.""That's amazing."

My mother would always see everything for everyone in the house. She wasn't good at sewing and she didn't care for it. But it needed to be done, and she did. She would take forever to see anything. My guess is that she tried putting it off as long as she could; or maybe she was too tired because she had to cook, clean and do chores outside as well.

"I like the color brown of your hair."

The youngest of the two women, smiled and playfully played with her hair. "Thank you, we did have blonde hair like yours, but we like the color brown more." "Did you change the color of your hair?" "Yes."

"Yes." The oldest spoke up, "We can't wear anything other than green, but our king didn't say we couldn't change our hair colors. " "We used coffee grounds." "Coffee grounds?"

I looked at my hair, the king and the king's men would surely find me with my blonde hair. "Can you show me? Do you know how to cut hair too?"

The oldest woman jumped and smiled, "I can dye your and my sister Rose, will cut your hair." "Perfect! What is your name?" "Mary."

Mary and Rose both took a side of my arm, we walked arm to arm all the way to their small house in the village. It was small and cold. Reminds me of my home with my parents. They have dress and shirt other clothing hanging up around in the house. Normally at my parents house they would do that if the clothes were drying and it was raining outside. They must be finish washing the clothes or finishing dying them.

"Sorry they are hanging because they need to dry off. We just dye them and soon to be sold. In the next couple of days we can try to sell them in the village." "Wow, that's amazing."

Mary told me to sit down, Rose began to cut my hair with her sewing scissors. She cut my long beautiful blonde hair to my shoulders. I don't even remember when my hair was ever this short. As long as I can remember my hair as always been long. A single tear came down my cheek.

"I didn't hurt you? Did I?""No, no. I never had my hair cut before. I love it."

I now feel like someone else, that I can be someone else. I don't feel like I have to worry about if someone would recognize me. Now I just have to let Mary dye my hair. I'm not sure how long the color of the coffee grounds would last but it gives me time to figure out if I'm going to stay here or go to the next kingdom. I could even take a ship and go even further away from Victor. I would need money for that.

While Rose washed my hair, Mary grounded up the coffee grounds in a fine powered, she said she bought in the market in the village in a few weeks ago. Mary and Rose also uses the coffee grounds to dye shoes, and other things. After she was done, Mary out the coffee powered on my damp wet hair.

The coffee smells burnt or bitter. I've never been a fan of coffee before. The smells always makes me what to throw up. My father would make it every morning before he would get outside and do his chores. I hated to smell it first thing in the morning.

Then Mary let the coffee powered stay on my hair for a while. I just sat still, I didn't want to move and something to go wrong. Rose said I could if I wanted to but I didn't want to. After a few minutes, Mary washed my hair out again. She said she could see the brown color in my hair. My hair is now officially short and brown.

Chapter 10
Dreaming of the future

Ivy's POV

I wonder if he, the king, could see me now if he could recognize me with my hair being brown and short. Mary, handed me a small hand mirror. I held the hand mirror in my hands. I couldn't believe my hair is brown now. Mary and Rose did great with my hair. I never had my hair done before. The ladies at the castle washed and brushed my hair. I wonder if queens and princesses feel after getting their hair done. I feel amazing, I feel powerful. Victor or anyone can't take this away from me, not even my father.

I remember, my mother would try to cut my hair every summer and my father would beat my mother for even cutting an itch off my hair. I don't want to live like that again. I want to be free to do what I want with my hair, and my body.

***

Later that night I helped Mary and Rose with dinner. We ate potatoes and green beans. It wasn't much but it was better than anything I ever had growing up. Since my family was always poor, we had to sell our vegetables that we grew. There wasn't much left.

A part of me does miss this castle. I don't miss the king or anyone in the castle. What I do miss is the food and wine. I'm sure Mary and Rose never had anything close to what I had at the castle. I wish things could be different, I wish Victor was different. Maybe I wouldn't mind being at the castle. I could grow to love it, I am sure I would. At least part of me is sure. Mary and Rose, has been so great to me. I wish things were different and I could bring them back with me.

Both Mary and Rose would love that my country you can wear whatever you want. They could open a shop and sell their beautiful clothes. I know I could get Victor to buy something from them. That would make everyone in the country want to buy clothes from them. They could even be the royal dress makers.

We ate dinner, Mary and Rose chatted with themselves about sleeping arrangements. Everything was still going around and around in my head. I kept thinking about the castle, Victor and if I do go back. I kept silent when helping clean the dishes. Since there are only two beds, Mary and Rose said they will share one bed and I can sleep on the other bed. I agreed and slipped on my nightgown and turned over. I closed my eyes and my mind was still racing about the thoughts I had during dinner.

I know I could never do something like that. I would have to make the king happy before he would do anything for me. If I do go back by willing or by force. He might kill me. They one word he could. With his mighty fist, he can kill anyone he wants. He never has to pay for his crimes. His crime.... He raped me, abused me, but he doesn't have to pay for his crime. He is king, his word is gold and even his actions. Victor is just a man just like anyone else. The kings need to pay for his crimes

If I ever do go back, I'll make sure he pays for his crimes. He's just a criminal with a crown. If he wants sex so badly with me; I'll make him pay for it. I'll bring him and his country to its knees.

***

I finally went to sleep. I slept like a baby, I never slept so good in my whole life. Sleeping in the castle was very comfortable but it wasn't much better than sleeping at home. At home, my father would make me wake up early and do my chores. Most of the time I would have to sleep on the wood floor. It was cold and dirty, and winter night was the worst. I could barely get warm. My feet would feel like falling off because it would be so cold, ice-cold. At the castle I wouldn't get any sleep because I worry that Victor would do something to me.

Chapter 11

Drawing Close

Victor's POV

She has been gone for three days. The festival is still going on. The festival will last two more days. How long is she going to be gone? I had this festival all planned out. What Ivy didn't know. I wanted to have our wedding on the last day of this festival or the day after the festival has ended.

I wanted it to be memorable for the wedding. I don't want the celebration to end. My people look happy and enjoy the day. Even the children are playing.

My knights and I are walking around in town. I want to be in the town with my people. I want them to see I am just a man, I was once one of them. It puts a smile on my face to see all my people enjoying themselves.

A group of small children ran past me holding a teddy bear, when I noticed a small little girl bumped into me. The small girl had tears running down her face. I bend down to her level, "What is wrong child?"

One of my knights spoke up, "Do you want us to remove her?"

I shook my head and motioned them to shoo away. I looked back at the little girl.

She wiped her face with the sleeve of her shirt, "They took my teddy." "Do you want me to get you a new one."

The little girl shook her head "no." I am still bending down to her level. "Do you still want that one teddy bear?""Yes.. Mr.Teddy!"

She smiled and just looked up at me. As if she was begging me to get it for her. I felt bad for the girl. She reminds me of the girl Vance used to play with when we were growing up. I never knew what happened to her.

I smiled and stood back up, I turned around facing the young boys. "Are you going to give back her teddy bear?"

The young boys looked terrified. The boys looked at me if I was going to bite their heads off. I grin, at this moment I can't laugh. Even if I wanted too laugh.

The oldest out of the young boys handed me the teddy bear. I looked at the teddy bear and then the young boys. I looked around, they noticed I was looking at them. The boys stood straight up.

One of my knights behind me, coughed to get my attention. "I'm sorry, your highness. The older one is my boy. The girl is my step daughter. I'm sure they were just playing around."

I handed the teddy bear to my knight. "Make sure she gets it.""Yes your highness."

I turned around to face the boys, the oldest of the young boys standing up tall. "You look like your father.""Yes your highness.""Do you plan to serve my kingdom like your father?""Yes your highness.""Great."

I patted the boy on the shoulder, when I went back to my knights that were guarding me. My knights and I smiled and went back to walk throughout the kingdom. The knight from before went to his step daughter to get her back her teddy bear.

***

My knights and I are sitting at my around table. Everyone is discussing the new updates on the rebellion that is happening in the smaller towns of the kingdom. We are hearing more and more cases of the rebellion getting closer to the kingdom.

I'm sure they want to take over the kingdom. But who could be behind the rebellion. I can't have King Leo to know anything about the rebellion. I'm sure he would back out of our treaty if he knew about the rebellion. He would think that I can't take care of my kingdom. I can't have that.

***

After my meeting with my knights, it's time for the feast of the festival. Every night of the festival we have a feast for everyone in the kingdom. Everyone gets to eat and drink on much they want. King Leo can have any women in the harem, if he wants. My royals of my court can have the woman of the harem too. If Ivy was here she would be with me, only me. The only woman in this kingdom I want.

***Ivy's POV

I turned over in my bed, I didn't see Mary and Rose in theirs. I quickly got out of the bed when I noticed I overslept. Mary and Rose made their bed, I made my bed before I looked around the small house.

I looked around the house. I didn't see the dresses hanging up from the night before. Mary and Rose must sell their clothes. I walked outside the house, Mary was talking to customers about the clothes. Rose makes sure the clothes are hanging in the right way for people to see them. From the looks of it, Rose is not as outgoing as Mary is.

***

I sat down watching them interact with customers. Mary is most of the talking. Rose made sketches of outfits. The sketches she was making were different from what they have been selling. Different colors and different fabric. I smiled, looking at her sketches.

"Do you like them?""Yes, they are very pretty.""Maybe one day you can wear one of them."

Mary turned around after she was done talking to a customer about the prices on a pair of pants, "We should close up shop for today, and get more apples. I want apple bread for dinner.""Dinner?""Yes."

We all agreed and I helped Mary and Rose put everything that was left that wasn't sold today back inside the small house. We hung the clothes up, Rose grabbed a wooden basket.

After everything was put inside the house, then Mary, Rose and I walked to the tree. Mary and Rose skipped their way to the tree, while Rose was still holding onto the wood basket. Mary smiled at me, "Here come hold hands with us."

I held Mary's hand, the three of us held hands while skipping to the tree. Mary, and Rose stopped in their tracks. Mary and Rose kept looking at the crowd of people.

"This doesn't look good. Everyone does gather around the tree. Not like this. Something must be going on."

We walked closer to the crowd, I noticed there were knights from my kingdom, and the knights were putting young girls in line.

I tried turning around and ran away. A knight with a drawing in his hand. Looked at me then looked at the drawing in his hand.

"You look like her. The girl's hair is different."

The knight is a few inches taller than I am, closer to Vance's height, same age as Vance too. The knight has brown hair and eyes with a hit of green. He has a little stubble on his face. He grabbed my arm and pulled me into the crown of young girls that he and the other knights were lining up.

Mary and Rose were in the same line of girls. Each knight looked each of the girls up and down. I turned my head to look at how many girls were in line. I counted 8 girls.

After the knights were done, look each girl up and down. A group of knights talking to each other in a small huddle. They looked at each one of us while they were talking. Not all the knights were in the huddle, three knights were in horses. With their hands on their swords. Everyone knows not to move. The knights could use their swords on us and kill us.

Each one of the girls does look like me in one way or the other. Same color eyes, same height or same size. Looking around at the girls, I think the knights are looking for me. I think the drawing that one of the knights is holding. Is a drawing of me.

One of the girls, when one of the knights wasn't looking at their horses. She made a run for it, towards the woods. One knights on a horse took off after her. She tripped on a rock and fell. She looked up at the knight, it looked as if she hurt her ankle. The knights took his sword and cut her neck. Blood is everywhere.

All the girls held onto each other, the knight with the drawing in his hand called out, "That will happen to you if you decided to run away."

All the girls looked at each other and cried. None of us wants to be here, but none of us wants to die. We knew we had better follow directions to stay alive.

Each knights to a girl and tied her hands to one long rope. The knight has the drawing in his hand, he folded the drawing, then put the drawing in his pouch on the side of his horse. He climbed up onto his horse and pulled on the rope that wrapped around our wrists.

The seven of us girls cried out when he pulled on the rope. He did that to make sure the rope was tight enough. The knight in front pulled on the ropes again and started to walk with his horse, pulled the rope while he started to walk in the direction of my kingdom.

Chapter 12
Without Warning

It seemed like hours the Knight on the horse pulled on the rope, each of the seven of us cried out in pain. Our wrists are bruises, swollen, raw and mine are bleeding now.

Each step we made to the castle my heart sank, I did this to Mary and Rose. I should've kept going. None of this would've happened. Mary and Rose would've lived happily in their small home and selling their clothes. Mary and Rose were happy before they met me.

One way, I'll get them back to their house and get them away from here. I know Mary and Rose, won't be happy here in this kingdom. Once they meet Victor is all over, I must get them out of here, or at least make it easier for them to live here.

***

After hours of walking, we finally reached my kingdom. The streets are empty, my guess they are having the festival. I overheard a few maids talking about getting everything prepared before I left. I looked around, and wanted posters of me all over the kingdom.

We reached the castle, the knight on the horse jumped down from his horse and pulled on the rope. Another knight pulled the horse to the back of the castle. If only Mary, Rose and I can squeeze out of these ropes, I can take one of the knights horses and run away from here.

Two knights were guarding the dining room doors. The knights opened the door. The knight pulled everyone into the dining hall. I looked around and all the King's men and townspeople, even the royals of the court; even the King Leo I met before I ran away, all standing still. The whole room went silent when we went into the dining room. Victor sitting on his chair in the middle of the dining room. Everyone looked at him for orders on what to do or say.

Victor didn't have any women hanging onto him like King Leo. He has three ladies from the harem hanging onto him. I only slightly looked up at Victor. I didn't want him to notice me. Maybe with my hair short and a different color he won't realize it's me. I can only hope that's the case.

The knight with one hand holding our rope, he took his other hand and pulled out the drawing, "My men and I found all the women that look like the woman in the wanted poster."

I hid my face in the shoulder of the girl standing beside me. Victor looked at the seven of us girls, then replied to the knight. "Most of them don't have blonde hair." "Yes, your highness."

The girls looked at Victor, I hid my face, while he walked in front of the seven of us. Victor looked closely at the girls in front of the line. The knight yelled for everyone to look forward. I still hid my face, one of the knights held the back of my neck to make me face forward. I screamed out in pain, then turned around and kicked the knight on his foot. The knight pulled my hair to make me look forward.

When I looked forward, Victor was standing in front of me. With one look he noticed me. I just stood there in silence and in horror. I dared not to say anything. It could get me killed and the girls that's tied to the rope with me.

"I have found her. Untie her. Right now!"

The knight that pulled my hair did what his king told him to do. He untied my ropes around my hands.

"What do you want us to do with the rest of the girls? Your highness?" Victor spoke up, "Take them to the harem."

"You can do anything you want with me. Just spare the girls."

The girls huddled behind me, crying and sobbing. I couldn't let Mary and Rose be in harem.

"Please! I beg you!"

Victor looked at me then the girls, "you can only spare two girls." "Mary and Rose" "They will be your maids."

The knights untied their ropes, I hugged Mary and Rose, they hugged me back. You can see Mary trying not to cry, but Rose already had tears in her eyes.

Without warning, he drags me into the hallway. He yells back to the crowd, "Please enjoy, I'm retiring early. I know I sure will."

You could hear people picking up their Instruments and starting to play music. People are laughing and chatting. I could barely hear them because I was screaming and kicking Victor to let go of my hair. We walked through the hallways and up the stairs. Every guard bowed to their king. I screamed for help. But there was no point. I screamed till we came to the bathhouse. The bathhouse in the up stairs are for the royals, kings, Victor.

Without warning, he did say anything. He grabbed my hair and by force he made me get into the bath. He didn't let go, I screamed and kicked and kicked. Clothes and all I made him wet from kicking the water.

He's going to kill me. He's going to drown me in the bathhouse! "STOP! STOP!""Hold still!"

I can feel my lungs fill up with water. I kicked and kicked, he came into the bath with me with one hand, the other holding onto me. He poured soap on my hair and scrubbed my hair. He scrubbed so hard it hurt my scalp.

"STOP STOP!"

I screamed, he kept scrubbing my hair. I tried moving away, he pulled my hair back. I fell into the water again, he dumped my hair back into the water over and over again.

He let go of my hair, I lifted up out of the water. Wiped off the water with my hands. I wrapped my arms around myself. The water was freezing cold, I started to shiver. Victor was all wet, from head to toe from me wetting him with the water. If I wasn't scared and shivering I would've laughed. This is not the right time or place.

He stood there looking at me smirking. I could smell the coffee that Mary and Rose used on my hair. The water turned the same color as my hair did. Victor's hands are slightly discolored from washing my hair out.

My hair is dripping down, how short my hair is now. I could only slightly see my blonde coming back from my hair. He was washing my hair out...

He moved closer to me, I jumped out of the bathtub and I ran for the door. Victor forcefully dragged me into the hallway, we walked to his room. Two guards straighten up, "This is my room. Don't let her out boys!"

We walked into his room, his room was elegant with silk blankets and pillows, with fur rugs on the ground and a fur blanket on the bed.

"I can't trust you to be in your own room till we are married. You are going to stay here while I keep an eye on you." "Please let me go." "Why did you leave?"

Victor's POV

I have to know why she left me. Why did she have to leave? She knows how much I love her. She knows how badly I need her. Ivy going to be my wife.

"I wanted to get away from you. Far as possible."

How can she hurt me, so I don't understand. She evokes feelings in me that I never knew. The gods had given her to me, and she will be forever mined. The gods will bless our union soon.

Ivy's POV

I saw the hurt and anger in his eyes. I know I hurt him when I said those words. How badly he has hurt me. I don't care if I hurt him with my words. He had hurt me in many ways, more than I never knew anyone could.

"Mark my words Ivy, you will never get away from me."

He ran over to me, his cold eyes, gripping my face harder, as tears formed in my eyes. He pushed into the doors. The guards on the other side know not to open the doors.

"Why did you have to leave!"

He punched the door, then I flinched when I felt his hand hold my cheek in a tender way, I looked up confused as to why he didn't hit me.

He could hurt me, punch me, beat me for running away, but he is holding my cheek in a tender way... I don't understand.

He moved away from me, then pulled a cream color night dress out of one of his drawers.

"Put this on and get on the bed."

I nodded, turned around and not facing him. I quickly took off my wet clothes and put on the night dress. Victor did the same, he took off his wet clothes and just changed his bottoms.

"Now get on the bed!"

I stood there, I didn't move. He's going to rape me like he did before. He's going to punish me for running away.

He walked closer to where I was standing, I was scared to even move. He reached out and grabbed a fist full of my damp hair. His grip firm, pulling me to him. I whimpered, then he yanked my hair back, forcing me to look up. Victor stared down at my chest.

Victor's POV

The outfit looked even better on her then I thought it was going to, her body filling it out perfectly. Her eyes looked away from me, pissing me off. I clenched my hand full of her hair, earning another whimper. "Am I clear on that order?"

With my hand in hair, I pushed her onto the bed. Tears rolling down her face. She looked scared and terrified at what I could do to her.

I climbed into bed and wrapped the blanket around me then turned my back on her. She stared at me, saying nothing and doing nothing on top of the bed.

"Don't make me tie you to the bedpost, go to sleep!"

I feel annoyed. I don't know what to do about her. About the fact that she ran away. I'm thankful she's back to where she belongs. With me, and soon she'll be my wife. Our union will be blessed. Our kingdom will be happy. To have a beautiful ruler by my side. She could make me do anything she wanted me to do. But she doesn't know she has that power over me yet.

Tomorrow is a big day in our kingdom. I have to get up early for the festival. Tomorrow I will fight for my beloved.

Chapter 13

Fire

Ivy's POV

I rolled over to Victor's side of the bed. I didn't see Victor on his side of the bed. It was true Victor didn't do anything to me last night. He didn't put his hands on me once last night. After I did go to sleep, I did sleep peacefully.

My doors slowly opened, I sat up in my bed, and I held my breath. It's King Victor coming to hurt me or rape me, maybe even punish me for running away from him. I closed my eyes and continued sitting on the bed, to prepare for whatever fate has in store for me.

First I heard Rose then I heard Mary's voice, I quickly opened my eyes. Mary and Rose rushed to my side of the bed and hugged me tightly. I jumped up from my bed, then hugged them again.

"Why are you here? How did you get in here?" "We are your personal maids." "Really?"

I held both of their hands, and tears came down my face. Mary and Rose shouldn't be here. They should've had to serve me, I don't deserve to be served by anyone.

"Why are you crying?"

Rose asked me why I was crying. Why are they crying? What did Victor do to them?

"Because you guys shouldn't be here. I'm so sorry. I should've kept running.""No, the King has been very nice to us.""He has? Why are you guys crying?"

Both of them nodded their heads and smiled. Mary spoke up, "Because we are happy that the King didn't do anything to you. That you are safe!"

Rose smiles very sweetly, wiping away her tears with her sleeve, "We thought he might have killed you. We were scared to come into the room. We thought we might have seen you in your own blood on the floor or the bed. Even he might have hurt you badly for running away."

"I'm sorry, I should've run away after you did my hair. You and Mary wouldn't be here like this." "We are not mad at you""Really?""Yes. You should've told us what you were running away from .""I'm sorry."

We all hugged, Rose pulled away then pulled a folded letter out of her pocket. "Here, I almost forgot. He wanted us to give it to you."

I unfolded the letter then read it out loud to Mary and Rose. "You will have two knights accompanying you all times today. I gave your maids my permission to go into the town, you may join them. You dare leave the town, I will find you and you will be punished. Love Victor."

I rolled my eyes at the last part of the letter, when it said, "Love Victor.". Then I looked over at Mary and Rose,"Did you know about what it said?"

Rose giggled and Mary tried not to giggle like Rose. I shook my head and tried not to smile.

***

After a few minutes I told Mary and Rose to step out so, I could change for the day. Mary and Rose offer but I Insisted that I could change myself. I didn't need help changing my clothes, I'm not a child.

After I got changed, I walked out of the room. Rose, Mary and me walked out of the castle and then started to walk out to the town. I turned around because I felt like someone was watching me. It was Vance, I haven't seen him since he saved me and let me go. Beside him was the knight that held the rope while the seven of us girls cried out in pain. Remembering what Victor's letter said I will have two knights accompanying us to the town.

I tried not letting it get to me that Victor has two knights watching me. I can't do anything myself. He's probably afraid that I'll run away again. But he's right I would run away if I had the chance. I would take Mary and Rose with me. We would get away from this place.

I wonder why he would pick the knight beside Vance to help watch me. I wonder if the reason, if Victor feels like he can trust Victor and the knight the most. He was in charge of getting me back. The reason he picked Vance is obvious. He's his right-hand man and his brother. Out of anyone I bet Victor trusts Vance the most.

Mary saw me looking back at the knights, "Why are you staring at them? Do you know them?" "That's Vance and I'm not sure his name is. But he is the knight that held the ropes." "He's name is Sam."

"Wait. How do you know his name?"

Rose giggled, then Mary, Rose and I walked arm to arm to the town, while Vance and Sam the other knight walked behind us. Every year the festival is always a sight to see. I would only go to the festival every other year or so. My father wouldn't let me. I would have to sneak off to go.

Every year the festival arrived and the excited energy was contagious. We spent most of the morning finishing up our cooking and setting up the tables and blankets in the courtyard of the town. Where there was room for people and the King's men to dance, sing, play music and eat. The King and the men of the country would joust. I never liked seeing all the blood. This year Damian wanted to be doing the jousting, like every one of his friends. He wanted me to watch him.

Getting lost in thought, Mary and Rose pulled my arms into the flower shop. "We need to pick flowers for your room!" Mary and Rose giggled, I yelled back at Vance and the other knight. "Please wait outside, it's just a flower shop. I'll be right out."

Vance and Sam agreed to stand in front of the shop. While Mary, Rose and I looked in the shop. Mary and Rose looking at one side of the shop. I walked closer to the back of the shop. That's where the shopkeeper always has the best looking flower Is in the back.

No one's POV

A group of people are shopping, but no one knows the back of the shop is in flames. The shopkeeper is in the back of the shop passed out because of the smoke. The smoke slowly filled up the shop. Since the frame of the shop is wooden, the roof of the shop has caught on fire. Slowly everything is on fire. The whole shop is on fire.

When Ivy noticed the smoke she ran into the back room of the shop. Fire burst in front of her. She coughs and coughing, looking around to see if she sees anyone in the back. She didn't see anyone earlier when she did walk into the shop.

She was about to stop looking because she could barely see anything in front of her because of the smoke coming from the surrounding fire. She was about to leave the room when she heard a slight noise. She looked at the ground, she saw the shopkeeper's legs. Ivy couldn't let anyone die in a horrible way like this. She grabbed the shopkeeper, and she started pulling her out of the room. When a thick wooden pillar fell on top of her back, she didn't move, she fell unconscious. Trapping Ivy and the shopkeeper inside the back room.

Meanwhile, Vance and Sam were standing in front of the shop checking out a farm girl walking by. They stopped when they heard screaming coming from the shop. They opened the wood door and fire and flames came from inside the shop. Vance and Sam rush in and help people out of the building. Both knights carried out people trying to get everyone safely out of the building.

Sam and Vance rush back into the shop, Sam finds Mary and Rose passed out on the ground holding bluebells in their hands. Vance yelled out to Mary and Rose, "Where is Ivy?" He kept yelling and yelling. Sam has Rose's arms wrapped around his neck, she slowly opens her eyes. She points to the back of the shop. Rose closes her eyes again and falls unconscious. Sam rushes her outside, then puts her down safely, then runs back in to save Mary.

The shopkeeper slowly makes conscious again, but is still going in and out of consciousness. Every time she came to consciousness she would scream, "Help!" Ivy unconscious with the thick wooden pillar on top of her back.

"Help!" the woman screamed again and judging from the sound Vance, in his state of unarm, the brave knight ran to the back of the shop. Years of training told him to be cautious but his concern for a woman in danger urged him to make haste. He knew he had to save Ivy from danger.

When Vance ran to the back of the shop he saw a door and tried to open it. The door didn't open to his nudges, Then Vance crashed into the room and was shocked at the sight.

Vance saw a woman going in and out of unconsciousness and Ivy unconscious with the thick wooden pillar on top of her back. Sam ran into where Vance is. Sam grabs the shopkeeper, Vance tries to pull the thick wooden pillar off her back when he gets under the pillar to move it. Then he put all this strength into moving the pillar with his back. He moves the wooden pillar away, then he hunches in pain. He hurt his back in the process of moving the pillar.

Ivy's POV

Going in and out of consciousness, everything around me is getting hot and it's hard to breathe. I feel warm hands around me, trying to move me. It must be Victor trying to hurt me again.

"STOP! STOP!"

I kicked and screamed, then suddenly with one forceful tug, he tore the hem of my dress. Using the long torn piece of fabric to bind my wrist, the man threw me over his shoulder, holding my legs, so I won't kick him. Then the man walked into the sunlight. The townspeople screaming for more water, and people trying to help to get the fire out. I passed out, unconscious.

~~~~~~~~~~~~~~~~~~~~~~~~~~~~~~~

I hope everyone loved the chapter! The next chapter will take me a couple of days to write! A lot of interesting stuff take place in the next couple of chapters!

~Please check out my other book on here!

Chapter 14
Feelings

When I opened my eyes, I saw Mary and Rose beside my bed. Mary and Rose have their hands bandage up. I slowly moved around, I looked down and I saw my chest was bandaged up. I have on bottoms, but I'm not wearing anything but the bandage on my chest.

"Ivy! You're alive!""Ivy.""Yes I'm alive. I'm in a lot of pain. Oww."

I tried to move around, I could only sit up in my bed. "What happened?""There was a fire at the flower shop."

"A lot of people got burned.""How badly did I get burned?""A little on your back. If we keep it clean and new bandage on it then it shouldn't make scars.""Good. Good. I don't want to remember Victor saving me."

I rolled my eyes and crossed my arms on my chest. Rose and Mary looked at me, it looked like they did know what to say to that.

"Your mistaken Ivy. Vance saves you. Sam saved us. They pulled us out of the burn flower shop.""What are you guys talking about?"Both nodded their heads, "It's true."

If what Mary and Rose said is true then, Vance saved me twice now. He saved me from getting eaten by wolves and burning to death in the fire. Everything is slowly coming back to me. I think I did hurt my head because I don't remember everything. It would explain why I thought it was Victor that saved me not Vance.

I can't believe Vance would run into a burning building to save me. I can feel my checks are heating up and my heart beating fast. The only time this has happened is when I was with Damian. I think I might start having feelings for Vance.

Lost in thought, Mary and Rose talking to each other, we stopped when we heard a little commotion outside the doors, then the wooden doors flow open.

Victor came in while guards around him. The look on Victor's face frightened me. I don't know what to think of his demeanor. When he came in with his guards, I quickly covered myself with the blanket. I didn't want Victor or his knights to see me.

"Ivy, I just heard what happened! She is going to be okay?" Mary and Rose both bowed to Victor, "Yes your highness."

"How bad is it?" "She needs rest and to keep her bandages clean your highness."

They spoke to him, but they didn't dare to look up at him. I stared at him, I didn't say anything to him.

"Make sure there's no sign of infection."

When he said that, it was like something clicked in my head. I remembered something, something is important that I forgot what it was.

Victor has a sad worried look on his face. It almost made me feel bad for him. Then Mary and Rose looked up at him, he blushed, his face turned a sight pink. Then he looked at me, then he walked out of the room. His guards followed behind him, walking back to their place to guard.

Rose first looked at Mary then at me, then she started to giggle, "I think he likes you. I think he really does care for you." "I think he has a hard time showing it, but yea I think so too. I agree with Rose."

"Finally you guys agree on something."

Everyone laughed, because they would not agree on anything when we were at their house. I scooted down into the bed, "I think I need some sleep."

***Flashback

My mother wanted me to find some herbs in the forest. The rest of my family went to the town to sell the eggs and whatever my mother grew in her garden. My mother thought it would be best if I could find herbs that we could eat, or we could sell. Food is scarce because of the war. Many nights we have gone hungry.

The old King has ruined this country because of his greediness. My father always says, "That damn King's greediness. He only wants glory and money. He's money hungry and the kingdom doesn't need another war but too many men are fighting in the war. We won't have a country if he keeps this up."

My mother said once my father served in the last war, when I was a baby. It changed him. He has never been the same. He didn't hurt his leg. That's why he needs the cane to walk.

***

Lost in thought I forgot back home I needed to clean out the barn before my family gets back from town. I grabbed my wooden basket with herbs. I hurried back to the family's farm. I heard the animals in the barn making noises, normally the animals are pretty quiet. There might be another snake in the barn making the animals go crazy.

I opened the one side of the barn's doors. What I stumbled upon I wasn't ready to see. He was laying down on a haystack. I looked over at him and studied him before I came closer to him.

The man was unconscious, maybe in his late 20 early 30. He was tall with broad shoulders. His clothes were torn, he must be a part of the knights that's fighting in the war. Why is he doing so far away from the castle? We Live miles away from the castle or even the town. He has a bruised face, and a long gash across his chest. I wonder if he is still alive.

I slowly moved closer to the man, putting my hand on his chest. I noticed he still had a heart beat but it's fast, I think he has a fever. He looks like he's on death's door.

I started to rip strips of cloth from the bottom of my dress. I ran over to the small spring where we get water every morning to feed the animals and water the garden. The spring water felt cool, I dipped the strips in the water then rang out the rest of the water.

Hopefully the cool water will bring down his fever. I ran back over to him with the strips of cloth, then I went back over to him. He was still unconscious, I took the strips of cloth and I cleaned the grime away off the man's face as best as I could.

When I wiped the grime away, I could help but to think he does have a handsome face. Even if he has one swollen eye and his lips were busted and raw. A strong chin, cheeks rough with hair and a little shallow as if he had not eaten for days.

I saw his gray eyes slowly open, "What are you doing? Who are you?""My name is Ivy. What is yours? Are you a part of the knights that have been fighting in this war?""Yes, Victor. My name is Victor. I am a knight for his highness. I must get back to the.... castle."

The man passed out unconscious again. I examined the long gash across his chest for infection. I didn't see any sign of infection. I said a quick prayer to myself, then cleaned around the gash she placed a dry strip of cloth on it.

I looked after him in the barn for two days. I nursed him back to health, I even gave him food and water. Whatever I could to get him back on his feet again. He would still go in and out of consciousness. I didn't tell anyone about him. I knew my father would beat me with the cane if he knew. Or he would the man with his cane.

End of Flashback ***

I woke up Mary and Rose still beside my bed, one is reading a book and the other one is drawing clothes on a notepad. I don't know if that was a dream or a flashback, maybe even both. Why would he be obsessive now? After I nursed him back to health?

That was 3 years ago, when I found him like that. He became king shortly after that and the war was over. Everyone lives happily after that, and a year after meeting Victor in my family's barn I met Damian.

I'm sure Vance wouldn't do anything like that. Vance is gentle and caring. I believe Vance is a good person. If he's willing to run into a burning building for me, then he's good, unlike his brother.

Chapter 15

Jealousy

I started to get out of my bed. Mary and Rose stopped what they were doing, "What are you doing?"

"I want to get out of bed and see the joust." "Ivy, you need rest." "I'm fine. I want to see it."

Rose and Mary helped me get into a new dress. I still have the bandage on my chest. I told them it was a little tight because of the bandage, they let the dress out a bit in the back. So it would be easier for me to breathe.

***Vance's POV

I promised myself that if Ivy came back I would win her affections and steal her away from Victor. Now she can be mine. I can take her away. Saving her twice now she's closer to becoming mine. Victor will have no chance of getting her back. Victor might have her body, but I will have her heart and soul. Then soon after I'll have her body too.

My squire has been busy making sure that my horse and armor is ready for the joust. I jumped on my horse, then my squire gave me my helmet, I looked at my helmet. I discovered that my helmet required some minor repairs since my last tournament.

I handed my helmet to my squire. "Tend to it, Henry." "Yes, sir."

He bowed and I saw Ivy and her two servants walking behind her. Her pink dress brings out her beauty. How the sun is shining on her makes her look even more beautiful.

Victor's POV

Every year we have the festival. The joust is my favorite part of the tournaments. I've been busy lately with everything being King I don't get to train with my knights. This is a fun way to train with them and I can fight for my beloved.

The joust makes me think of simple times. My squire and the squires remind me of when Vance and I were younger. Normally sons born of noble families and who were slated to become knights were sent away at the age of seven to live in the house of a lord or uncle. There, they would become pages and begin their knight training.

It was possible (but not common) for a man of ignoble birth to become a knight by performing courageously on the battlefield. But for Vance and I were orphans. A lord found us and took us in. He raised us, he was like a father to us. He's the man I want to be. Even if he had a taste for young women and drink. He taught me everything I know.

At the age of fourteen, Vance and I began as a page then we became squires, and then we apprenticed under a knight under the old king. The knights that we did appreciate under died the night I became knight. I remember him being strict, but he wanted us to be the best knights we could be.

As Vance and I were squires, we trained constantly so our bodies were perfect weaponry skills. Many boys were winnowed out during the squire stage because the training was so difficult. Vance and I were the perfect simple squires, even if we got into trouble many times. Squires who made it through the training program were usually knighted around the age of 21. Vance and I became knights at 21.

A squire's responsibilities included helping the knight get dressed, taking care of the knight's horse, serving the knight food, and cleaning and polishing the knight's weapons and coat of armor. The cost of armor, weapons, horse, and shield, becoming a knight was extremely expensive. You had to take good care of your belongings. Squires are taught how to take care of the knights belongings on day one. A full suit of plate armor weighed more than 50 pounds, but because the weight was evenly distributed all over the body, armored knights had remarkable mobility.

The purpose of tournaments was originally to train for battle, but since the losers often had to give up their horse and armor to the winner. In my kingdom, the winner gets a bag full of coins, and a kiss from anyone in the kingdom. Widowed, young, old, a part of the harem or not.

Mostly the church is not in favor of tournaments since many players were injured and killed. The churches in my kingdom agreed to look away if no one gets killed for a fee.

***

As my squire gets my horse and armor ready for the tournament. I see Ivy and her two servants walking behind her. I couldn't help but to smile. My beloved Ivy is giving me a token for luck. A token is usually a lady's ribbon or handkerchief that she gives to a knight of her choice or a joust. It is said to bring the knight luck.

I will surely win if I have Ivy's token.

Ivy and her two servants stop at where Vance is getting ready for the tournament. I walked closer to where they were standing, I hid behind some hay. Vance looks happy to see Ivy. Ivy is smiling and blushing. Her cheeks are pinker than her dress. Her two servants behind her are giggling about the situation. None of them are aware that I am seeing everything.

I was about to walk over there when I saw Ivy give her handkerchief to Vance. My blood is boiling with anger. I'll make sure he doesn't win this tournament if it's the last thing I do and I'll make sure Ivy gets punished for betraying me.

Chapter 16

Warning

Victor's POV

I'm still hiding where I was standing, I can see everything. Ivy looks happy as she can be. Like when she was with Damian. I got rid of Damian with one swing of my sword, I can do the same to Vance. Even if he's my brother, he knows better than to get in my way of what I want.

For this time I'll give him a warning shot, if he doesn't back off then I'll have to do it. I don't want to but if he doesn't back off, I will. I'll have to kill him.

***

Everyone in the town cheering for their favorite knight. Many people are cheering my name. I look up to where Ivy is, she's sitting down next to my chair. Where the royals and people of the court are spectating. King Leo is spectating the tournament today.

I have been joust with many knights, the last joust for today is with Vance. After this joust whichever is the winner gets a bag full of coins, and a kiss from anyone in the kingdom. Widowed, young, old, a part of the harem or not. I want more than just a kiss from Ivy. Special because she hurt me. She's going to get more than just a kiss.

Sitting on top of my horse in full armor, I'm holding my helmet. My horse has my family's crest; it's a crescent moon. My family's colors are white and blue. My squire is holding my lance. My lance at the end point is a skull.

Each knight has different colors to represent their families name. Even the end of the lance is different. The end of Vance's lances an arrowhead. He's horse is wearing our family's crest and colors.

As my squire is pulling my horse to where I am supposed to be starting from. I couldn't help but to stare at Ivy, she turned her head and smiled at the opposite side of me at Vance.

Ivy staring at him makes my blood boil even more. She should be cheering for me. I should have her token. I look around, I see my knight and their loved ones. The ladies are giving the knights their tokens. My heart feels like it's screaming at me. Screaming for Ivy. I'm hurt and angry.. Vance is going to pay.

As Vance gets read on the other side, my squire gives me my lance. I line up my lance right for his heart. He made my heart hurt, I will do the same. I don't care if it kills him or hurts him. I told my squire not to use my lances with poison in it. Those lances have poison in them. After the skull is broken off, then the poison will kill you.

My squire hands me my helmet. As Vance smiles and waves to the cheering crowd of people. I slam my helmet shut, and recheck my angle of my lance. As I take one look at Ivy before, the green flags go down. I look straightforward.

The green flag drops, I kick my heels for my horse to run straightforward to Vance. Vance and his horse do the same. His lance barely hits my shoulder. My lance almost knocked him off his horse, and destroyed his lance. The crowd is cheering and his face looks shocked. He wasn't expecting me to hit him so hard. Brother or not I will give him everything he deserves.

"Round one goes to.... King Victor!"

The crowd goes wild as Vance and I go back to where we started from. The joust has three rounds. It can go into a sudden death if we both win the third round. We would both have to fall off of our horses. It's an automatic win if someone dies.

The green flag drops again, I kick my heels for my horse to run straightforward to Vance for the second time. Vance and his horse do the same. His lance hits my shoulder. My shoulder is now out of place.

My lance hit his lance and ricochets and hits him in the eye. Blood coming down from his face. The crowd is cheering and gasping at the site. Gasping at the blood. I look up at Ivy, she's more worried about Vance than me. This makes me even more angry at Vance and Ivy.

Vance and I go back to where we started from. The doctors are checking both of us out. For my out-of-place shoulder and Vance's right eye.

"Round two goes to.... King Victor!

I pop my shoulder back into place. Vance gives the okay that he's going to compete in the next round. I smirk to myself, and give Ivy a quick wink. I line up my lance right for his heart.

The green flag drops again for the last time, I kick my heels for my horse to run straightforward to Vance for the third time. Vance and his horse do the same. Before Vance's lance has a chance to hit me, with all of my force in my lance, Vance falls off of his horse. His squire runs up to him and says he has been knocked unconscious.

"The winner is.. King Victor!"

The crowd goes wild as they hear my name. Ivy saw what happened and she ran for Vance. I quickly got off my horse. A royal hands me the coins for winning the tournament. I throw the bag at the crowd of people. My people need the coins more than I do. The only thing I want is Ivy. I see, Ivy runs to him and gets down on her knees where Vance is.

I quickly pulled Ivy's arm, "It's time for me to claim my prize." I squeezed her arm in my hand. Ivy trying to remove my hand. "Please let me care for him!""You can flirt with him again, I don't think so."

***

Ivy screamed and tried to scratch me. We made it into castle and up the stairs. I squeezed even harder and dragged her into my room. I yelled for the guards outside my room to not let anyone disturb us.

Chapter 17
Punishment For Your Betrayal

"Let go of me!" "Never!" I screamed at her then I threw her on top of the bed. I ripped her pink dress, the front of her corset exposing her beautiful perky breast. She kept screaming and kicking me. I put her wrist together, and held her wrists with one wrist. With my other wrist I traced her body until I cupped her breast in my hand then I licked her left nipple.

"I'm going to be strict and discipline you well, so you won't ever betray me again." "I didn't betray you!" "You gave your token to Vance or you don't remember that."

She stopped wiggling around, "You hurt him on purpose, didn't you?"

I licked her neck then sucked in her sweet skin. "Yes. That was a warning. Next time you flirt with him, I will kill him or any man." He's your brother!" "No one stands in my way!"

"No! No! He's your brother!"

With my hand still holding on her wrist, she kicked me right in the balls. I let go on her wrists, she quickly got off the bed and ran to the doors. I held onto my balls in pain.

She tried to open the doors, but I explained to the guards from now on. The doors must stay closed until I say open them. When I give them my word, then they will open the doors. She doesn't know I already have my orders after she left.

She kicked and screamed for them to open. The guards wouldn't open the door. I held my balls, trying to relieve the pain. I could also hear Ivy's two servants begging the guards on the other side of the door to open. Their voices were so loud I could hear them over Ivy's screaming.

With the doors still closed and Ivy holding onto the handle, I turned Ivy around to face me. I pushed her against the door. Ivy started to shake in fear. I pulled her waist to me, then whispered into her ear, "If you want to trade places with your servants. I'll take both of them tonight. They will hate you forever because I won't show mercy on them." "You wouldn't dare."

I licked her ear then nipped on her ear, "I would." "Please don't." "It's you or your friends." "I will." "Freely?" "Yes."

"Are you sure you want to do this?" "Yes."

A single tear came down her face. I knew if I threatened her friends, she would say yes. For once, she is giving herself to me freely. My one wish is for her to give herself to me freely. All of her body and soul. Even her womb.

***

Ivy stared straight at me with no emotion on her face, then she slightly pushed me away to move away from the bed. She climbed on top of the bed, removed her ripped clothing. I removed my clothes and climbed on the bed.

I climbed in between her legs. Normally she would kick and scream at me at the moment, she's not. She just looked straight at me. I started to kiss her, "Kiss back."

She kissed back, I kissed her neck then collarbone. She wrapped her legs around me, I smirked to myself. She must be enjoying her herself for once. I started kissing her neck then moving down to her breast. I started licking and sucking on her left nipple then moving to her right nipple. She started to moan, she bit her finger to stop.

"If you keep it up with moaning, it won't be a punishment."

I smirked, then she rolled her eyes at me. Her face turned a slight pinkish. I went to kiss her again, while my right hand traveled down to her private area. I sucked on her neck making hickies. While moving my fighters in her private area in and out. She tried not moving or making any sound.

Making hickies on her neck, remind me we are not here to make love. She's here for a punishment. I moved my body down. I held onto her legs, I kissed and sucked on her inner thighs. She tried moving my head away for me to stop. I kept on going. She ran her fingers through my hair. If she was here to make love I would be happy to explore her private area with my tongue.

"Please stop." "No. You are mine tonight."

I left wet kisses on her inner thighs, then moved my body in between her legs, "Wrap your legs around me."

She nodded and wrapped her legs around my waist. I looked her straight in the eyes when I went in. She slightly arched her back, when I went in. She tried not to moan again.

***

I fucked her in the same position for hours. I looked over to the candles. The candles that were freshly lit when came into the room, are almost burnt out. The candles made me have an idea. Another way to punish her.

While I kept going in and out of her, with one hand I grabbed the candle and poured the candle wax on her nipples. When she screamed out in pain, it was almost a moan. It's like her body is getting used to my touch and the dirty things I do to her.

With her moaning and screaming, it made me spill my seed into her. I kissed her lips softly, she didn't kiss back. It made my heart hurt. I thought she was enjoying herself. Maybe not enough. After removing myself from inside her, I kissed her on the stomach.

Soon.

***

I grabbed my robe and put it on. Ivy sat up in the bed and kept staring at me, holding onto the blanket to her chest. I moved off the bed, I was about to tell the guards to open up.

I turned back to Ivy, "Just know this, I went easy on you. If you run away from me again..I'll break your legs."

She looks scared and frightened. Good. I want her to realize she can't run away from me. Her home is here with me. Her womb is filled with my seed and only by my seed. After we are married, she'll have my babies. We can be a happy family.

Chapter 18
Dancing? Rebellion?

Ivy's POV

Victor left the room, I was still sitting up on the bed holding the blankets to my chest. Right after Victor left the room, Mary and Rose came through the door. The guards shut the door behind them.

Rose holding a new dress in her hands. She put a green dress across the bed to lay it out so it wouldn't get wrinkled. Mary and Rose walked closer to me, "Are you okay?" "We tried screaming for you." "What did he do to you?"

I hugged myself with the blankets. I can smell the scent on the blankets and on me. My cheeks went hot and I bit my lip.

"I'm fine, don't worry."

I wonder why they brought in a new dress? I've never seen it before. I do love the color and the design of the dress.

"Why did you bring in the dress?" "It's for the ball! King Victor said we could enjoy the festivities. I'm so excited."

Mary crossed her arms, "I don't want to go to the ball. I would rather be at home reading a book."

Rose playfully pulled on Mary's arm, "Please come to the ball, I can't go by myself. Ivy is going to be with the King and I'll be by myself. Plea—seeee."

"Okay okay, don't do that again."Rose jumping up and down in excitement, "Yay!"

"Okay, let's get Ivy ready for tonight.""Okay."

I nodded and removed the blankets from my chest. Mary and Rose were shocked to see that I have candle wax on my chest and hickies on my neck, legs, chest. They could see what he did to me while they begged the guards to open the door.

"He's a monster."

Rose covered her mouth looking at my body. A single tear came down her face. Mary grabbed the blanket off the bed to cover myself with.

"Let's bring her to the bath."

***Unknown POV

Everyone in the room received the same message to meet here. Our leader paid a farmer to use his barn. The farm is letting everyone that knows the password inside the barn. He's not the only person in the country that agrees with us. Our rebellion is getting stronger and stronger every day. Soon our leader will take the crown and bring this country to its knees.

Everyone is standing and sitting around waiting for our leader to come to start the meeting. I always stand in the back, but I am our leader's right-hand man. I don't talk much, I watch and listen. My job is to make sure everyone in the rebellion is going to follow our leaders orders. No one makes a move without our leader's decision.

I stood in the back of the barn listening to everyone's conversation. I noticed the farmer quickly opened the door to the barn. Everyone in the barn quickly got on the feet. Our leader is covered in blood and cuts. He has his left arm in a bandage.

Someone yelled, "What happened to you?""It doesn't matter what happened to me. It's time. We can't wait any longer. Who agrees? Say "I."

Everyone in the barn said,"I." Men, women and children. One woman walked over to him and cleaned him up more. She's always sweet on our leader. Now it's time to start the plan to take over the kingdom.

***The BallIvy's POV

The guards escorted me to the ball. Tomorrow is the big hunt. Victor and his men are going to be gone away from the castle for a few days. It will be good to be away from Victor. What happened earlier can't happen again. I will fall for him if it does. I don't want to. Maybe soon I can still get away from this place and bring Mary and Rose with me. Maybe soon Victor will get bored with me and let me go.

The guards opened the doors then I looked around and everyone in the room was smiling and laughing, all the King's men and townspeople, even the royals of the court. A few people are playing Instruments and playing music. The music sounds lovely.

Even the King Leo is smiling and laughing with someone. This time he didn't have three girls from the haram all over him. He only has one. Walking closer to her, she looks familiar like I have seen her before.

Walking closer to them I noticed she was one of the girls that was forced to come here. She was behind Rose in the lineup. She still doesn't look happy, she mostly looks scared. King Leo is drinking his wine and with the other hand softly playing with the tips of his fingers with her brown hair. She jumps in her seat every time he gets a piece of her hair and smells it.

I wish I could help here but I can't. I don't have that power over Victor for him to do anything I ask him too. The only thing I did ask him is to not let Mary and Rose be a part of the haram. At least he did do that, I am grateful.

When the doors opened, the whole room went silent when we went into the dining room. Victor slowly stepped up the small stairs leading up to the throne, and turned around to face his audience. Everyone in the room bowed, including me.

King Leo turned to him and started to talk with Victor. I turned away and tried to scan the crowd for Vance, I couldn't find him. I see Mary and Rose having a good time smiling, laughing and dancing with two royals.

I walked over to the table of food and wine. A grabbed a cup of wine. I walked afterwards to the balcony for some fresh air. At least none of the knights are guarding the balcony. I know Victor can keep his eyes on me from his throne.

I walked to the end of the balcony and smelled the fresh air. It smells like it's going to rain. It's my favorite smell, the smell of rain. I stared up at the moon. The moon looks big tonight, like you could pull the moon closer and touch it. It's a beautiful night. I sipped on the wine and stared straight up at the moon.

I wish I had someone to share this moment with. Someone I don't have to be scared of. I can relax and be myself. Someone I can really fall in love with.

Sipping on my cup of wine I felt warm arms wrap around my waist. Maybe I could get used to Victor's warmth. Maybe I could in the future feel safe with him, "Victor stop."

I turned around with his arms still wrapped around my waist. Vance spoke up, "Wrong brother.""Vance?"

I slightly pushed him away from me, "What are you doing here?""You're not thinking about jumping are you?""No, I wouldn't dare."

"Good, then why are you here?""Oh, I'm just exhausted, I needed some fresh air."

"Yeah, I can see the bags under your eyes. You do look really tired .""It's been a long day."

"Run away with me. We can join the rebels and be part of the rebellion against my brother." "Rebellion?" "Yes, they are going to overthrow Victor. Might even kill him." "Wait, how do you know this?" "All the knights know. I thought you knew."

Someone walked out to the balcony and cleared their throat, I turned to face who it was. It's one of Victor's servants.

"Ivy, the King wishes you to speak to you."

I nodded, bowed to Vance. I walked over to where Victor was sitting down. He motioned for me to sit down beside him.

"Are you being good my dear?""Yes.""Dance with me."

Victor stood up and pulled my wrist to follow him to where everyone is dancing. The people playing the music, picked up their instruments and started to play.

"Do not worry about your feet...follow my movements."

He moved so elegantly across the floor, pulling me with him. I blushed and moved with him, then we started to move in sync, it felt like we were floating. I have never danced like this before.

"Look at me."

I stared up at him while me danced, "I saw your conversation with Vance. Do I need to remind you what I said earlier? Or do I need to make you remember?"

I could feel his warm hands on my waist, pulling me closer to him. My breast is closer to his chest. I tried to push his hand away, he kept pulling me closer to him while we danced.

"Tomorrow is the hunt. You don't want Vance to be in a hunting accident, do you."

He pulled away a little, so we were arms length apart, before he twisted me in a circle, pulling me back into his chest. I looked up at him, our eyes locked, sending shivers down my spine, his stare was cold and angry, his face hard. He pulled me closer to him, then he whispered in my ear, "Let's go to sleep."

I just stood there, I stopped dancing with him. He pulled my wrist and we walked to our room. The guards bowed as we walked by. Victor wasn't pulling me hard, he was pulling me, so I know he's serious. What is he going to do next? Is going to punish me for talking to Vance? I wonder if he knows what Vance said? Is it true?

***

The guards opened the doors when Victor gave his orders. We walked into the room, he let go of my wrist.

"Go to sleep."

He took off his clothes then climbed into bed. I undid my front corset of my green dress. I looked over to him. He turned over, with his eyes closed.

"I can ask you something?"

He opened his eyes, "Yes you may." "Do you know about the rebellion against you."

Without even a second to think about it, he said "Yes." So what Vance told me is the truth. There is a rebellion against Victor.

"Where did you hear that from?" "No..no one. I overheard someone talking about it." "Thank you for telling me. Climb into bed. I won't do anything to you, I promise. Tomorrow is busy today."

I nodded and climbed into bed. I do believe him when he said he won't do anything to me. At least part of me does. I don't trust him fully, probably never will.

"Thank you again for telling me. I know I can trust you... It is hard to actually trust people when you are in my position...the whole kingdom rests on my shoulders, if I make one move...it could be dangerous."

After he said that he turned over and went hard fast asleep. He must be tired and it must be tiring not to trust anyone in his position. I wonder how much he does trust Vance? I also wonder how much he trusts me?

~~~~~~~~~~~~~~~~~~~~~~~~~~~~~~

~I might create a new book with King Leo and his girl After I am done with this book... Yes or no

Chapter 19
The Royal Hunt

Ivy's POV

Victor stayed on his side of the bed, he didn't touch me once. I think I felt his lips on my forehead earlier this morning. It was light and gentle, I don't think that was Victor. I must have been dreaming. Victor could never be that gentle with me.

I sat up in my bed when I heard a knock on the door. The guards opened the doors, Mary and Rose came into the room.

"Mary, Rose I don't want to get ready for the day so soon. Since Victor and his men are going to be away, I want to relax today."

Mary and Rose looked at me then at each other, as if my head wasn't on right. "What are you talking about? The king sent us here to help you pack and to get you ready for the royal hunt."

"What?" "Yes, it's true. Even King Leo and his women are going."

***

Mary and Rose helped me pack for the hunt. I changed into a gray dress with short sleeves. Rose said that Victor told them that I needed to wear a warm coat. The early morning gets really cold outside. I put on my dress and my coat.

Mary helped to get me dressed, while Rose finished packing. Victor or the knights didn't tell them what I would need during my time at the royal hunt. She put in my wooden luggage what she thought I would need. Mary looked at my bandages, she thinks I don't need them anymore. The burns are healing up nicely, she doesn't think it will scar.

After Mary and Rose were done, a few knights walked into the room to grab my wooden luggage to put them on the carriage. Mary and Rose followed me outside.

Victor is sitting on top of his white horse, the horse and Victor is wearing his family's crest; it's a crescent moon. His family's colors are white and blue. His squire is packing things into the saddlebags on the side of the horse.

Victor's knights are on top of their horses too, I turn my head to Rose, and she is blushing. Both Mary and I looked at Rose, she's smiling at Sam. Mary and I giggled at Rose.

I looked around at the knights, I don't see Vance anywhere. I do see King Leo and his women. She looks sad and scared. I do hope one day I get to talk to her. Maybe I can get Victor to release the girl from King Leo's grip.

*** After the servants packed everything up, everyone got on their horses. Victor tied my horse to his. If his horse went fast, my horse went fast. When his horse stopped, my horse stopped. I still believe Victor still doesn't trust me.

He probably thinks I will run if I get the chance too. Now that I have a horse, I can easily run away from him. That thought did cross my mind.

The reason why I have to come with him on the hunt is because he probably thinks I would do the same thing at the castle. I would run away if I had the chance. If he's gone, I would have a chance to get away from him. Again, the thought did cross my mind.

It was only a thought, I still have to make Victor pay for his crimes. I still have to bring him and his country to its knees.

I looked over to Victor and slightly smiled at him. As Victor, his knights and a few servants and I walked on the path down to where we are supposed to be having the royal hunt. Victor looks very happy. I've never seen him like this before. I kept staring at him. He turned his head to me and looked at me, "Why are you staring at me?""Nothing."

If he keeps this up, I might start developing feelings for him. He may be rough on the outside but I think there is something about him that he only lets me see. Something that he's hiding but something is there. Something that I like about him. I will never tell him anything about it but I do. I like that part about him.

Victor snaps me out of my head, "Do you see that right there?"

Victor asked, pointing to a deer about ten feet away. A big mighty deer with big antlers. The deer is grazing on a small patch of grass that wasn't covered in the morning dew.

I watch, my breaths silent. Victor takes hold of his bow, snatches an arrow... aim... shoot.

The deer fell down. The servants go and pick the deer up.

We walked through the path and Victor spotted a duck flying by. Victor takes hold of his bow, snatches an arrow... aim... shoot.

Three more ducks fly by, and Victor takes hold of his bow, snatches an arrow... aims... shoots.

The four ducks fell down. Just like before The servants go and pick the ducks up.

Seeing Victor killing the poor ducks makes me feel nauseous. My father used to kill deer, so I used to see it. Not ducks, he never shot a duck, like Victor. I always love seeing the ducks on the pond, where my father used to hunt. I think we are close. He would stay in a little wooden house. Much smaller than our house surprisingly. I was really little the last time I went with him.

Victor saw the look on my face when I started to feel nauseous, "It's okay. It was quick, I promise. He's in a better place."

At least he tried to say anything that would make me feel better about what he's doing.

"Let's keep moving, we are almost to the stopping area!"

Everyone walked forward, the knights knew where they were going to stop. The royal hunt is supposed to last three days. From what I overheard the knights talking before left. They pick out a different spot every year. So no enemy can make a surprise attack.

"Sure," I mumbled, he must have heard it, because he chuckled." What don't you believe in heaven or a higher power?""No, I don't think I do. But I do believe in hell.""Where is hell?""With you."

He looked like I caught him off guard, then he smirked at me, "Heaven is in between your legs."

Now I feel like really throwing up. How can he talk about something like that. Doesn't he care that one of his knights or royals or even King Leo will hear him?

*** The horse and everyone walked forward after some time we made it to the campsite. This is the area that his knights picked out to be the spot where rest. The servants set up the campsite while Victor and his knights set out to hunt for animals. I set on my horse and waited till the campsite was finished.

That afternoon, everyone was eating, drinking and enjoying themselves around the campfire. Victor and Leo chatting about the kingdoms. His girl didn't look like she wanted to talk to me or anyone else.

I whispered into Victor's ear that I wanted to rest in our tent. He nodded and went back to his conversation with King Leo. King Leo smiled and nodded. I bowed to them, started to walk to my and Victor's tent.

I was about to go inside the tent when a hand covered my mouth, I felt a knife pointing at my back. The man pulled me away from my tent. I screamed out as loud as I could then everything went black.

Chapter 20

The Prey Part 1

Victor's POV

I heard Ivy scream; I know it's Ivy from the scream. I can spot her out of anywhere. She is not the type of girl to scream at a bug or a snake. It has to be something wrong for her to scream.

I jumped up from where I was sitting. I ran the direction where I heard Ivy scream. Our tent, she was going to our tent when I heard her scream.

I looked in our tent, Ivy was nowhere to be seen, "Ivy!" I screamed out her name. No answer.

I ran outside the tent, my knights standing around. They must have heard Ivy scream too, "Why are you standing around? Go find Ivy!"

One knight limping with blood running down his face, "They went that way. I tried to stop them, Your highness. I was attacked." He pointed in the direction of where they were going.

The knight tried to bow to me, but he fell on the ground. Two knights rush to his side and carry him to the servants to be bandages up. I turned to my knights, and screamed, "I want all of you to find Ivy! Take no prisoners!"

***

It's been hours since I heard Ivy scream. I've had my knights looking for her all night. The next morning, King Leo thought it would be best if we cut this hunt short and take everyone that's not needed to find Ivy back to the castle.

He was right, we can't risk anyone else be kidnapped. I can't have King Leo thinking I am weak. That I can't control my kingdom.

A small group of people rode back to the castle. I wanted to take this horse and ride off to find Ivy myself. I have no one to watch the kingdom for me. I needed to make sure King Leo was escorted safely back to castle.

***

We made it to the castle. My knights from. The search party hasn't come back yet. I walked into the throne room, I couldn't help but to pace back and forth in the room. Then one of my knights came in.

"Have you found her? Please tell me you found her!""We haven't. Your highness."

"Where is Vance? He needs to come here now!"

The knight bowed to me, with his head down, "Your highness. We have a problem... Also, Sir Vance is nowhere to be found.""What."

"There are fires everywhere. In your country your highness. We think it's the rebels.""That means, the rebels took Ivy. Have they taken Vance too?"

I walked around the throne room and threw everything I touched to the ground. Still pacing back and forth. Throwing things at the walls, on the ground.

I feel like I can't do anything for her or my people. As a king, I can't. My people need me and I can't help my people. Ivy needs me and I can't help her. I can't help anyone.

Where is my brother? Where is Ivy? They wouldn't have run away together. No... He wouldn't dare. He knows I would kill him if he touched her in any way. She knows I would kill her or make her wish she was dead.

The rest of my knights walked in and all the knights waited to hear my orders. With everyone looking at me. Even King Leo and his knights came into the throne room. King Leo and his knights stood behind my men.

"Who is our traitor? Come forward!"

My knights looked around at each other then back at me, "We have a traitor in our knighthood, me and only my knights knew where we were going to be hunting in which part of the kingdom... Which one of you is working with the rebels? With the rebellion to overthrow me?"

My knights looked around at each other then, back at me just like my first question, "I will find out who it is and I'll have his head on a silver platter...Every available knight needs to stop looking for Ivy, and put out the fires."

My knights walked out of the throne room. My heart sank. Ivy means the world to me. I would give her my last breath. I would die for her. My people need me too.

"King Victor, we need to talk."

King Leo walked up to me and put his hand on my shoulder, turning away from his head standing behind him.

"I will help you find her and my knights will assist with putting out the fires. We are allies. Agreed."

King Leo put out his hand to shake my head, "You can order my men as you wish. I want one thing in return." "What would that be?"

King Leo leaned closer to my year and whispered something. At first, I thought it was joking but from the look on his face, I know he wasn't. I know that look.

"Agreed."

King Leo and I shook hands, while shaking my head. He turned to his knights, "You follow his orders and his men. We are allies until this is over. Then we will discuss future partnership."

His knights cheered and walked out of the room. King Leo and I turned to each other and discussed our future partnership.

Chapter 21

The Prey Part 2

U nknown POV

The king sent out his men to scour the woods for any signs of where Ivy could be. The king sent the rest of his men to put out the fires in the rest of the kingdom. Even King Leo, sent his knights out to help. King Leo is trying his best to help King Victor.

Everyone in the kingdom is talking about the knighthood. The knighthood has a traitor in their knighthood. How could that be? How could King Victor let that happen?

The knights have always been well looked at. Everyone in the kingdom respects the knights. How could a knight betray his kingdom and his knighthood?

The rumors about whom it could have been spreading like wildfire. Everyone is running around in a frenzy because of the fires and the rumors. There are even rumors about people breaking into people's homes. No feels like they can trust anyone.

On top of everything everyone is chatting about king Victor is losing his mind over not being able to find Ivy. I do hope they can find that sweet girl. She seems like she would be sweet.

***Ivy's POV

The last thing I remember is, I was screaming then everything went black. I don't remember why or what for. Just darkness.

"Ivy wake up!"

I heard my name. The voice sounds so familiar. Like I recognize the voice. I heard that voice before.

I think I hit my head. My head really hurts. I feel dizzy. Really dizzy.

I tried opening my eyes, but some cloth was over my eyes. A cloth is covering my mouth preventing me from speaking. I noticed my hands are tied up with rope. I tried moving my hands to break free, but I couldn't. The ropes are tied too tight. The tightness of the ropes are hurting my hands.

"Ivy!"

I shook my head, I couldn't say anything. I couldn't speak. No words came out of my mouth. I felt a hand removing my cloth covering my eyes.

When I opened my eyes, I could see Vance. Why is Vance here? Is he here to rescue me like before? This would be the third time he has rescued me.

I tried screaming and trying to move to break from these ropes. Vance is standing in front of me. Why isn't he helping me?

He removes the clothes around my mouth, "Ivy?"

~~~~~~~~~~~~~~~~~~~~~~~~~~~~~~ Sorry for how short it is, but the next chapter is the big reveal!

Chapter 22
The Prey part 3

Ivy's POV

Vance standing in front of me calling my name. I must have hurt my head somehow. Everything is dizzy and I feel my head is spinning.

"What?"

Vance turned around to the man standing behind him, "Why did you hit her head so hard? Who told you to do that?" "No one sir. She was screaming. We didn't want to be caught."

Vance went up to him and punched the man right in the nose, "My orders were to bring her to me without being harmed in any way."

The man bowed, blood coming from his nose. Vance must have broken his nose, "It won't happen again sir." "Leave!"

My head is still spinning, my eyes can't focus on anything. I tried to look around to figure out where I am. I think I am in a barn. There's hay everywhere on the ground, it's a wooden structure like a barn. I'm sitting on hay with my hands tied with rope and my back is again a wooden beam.

Vance turned around to face me, "Vance save me.""I'm not here to help you."

I mustn't have heard him correctly, "Save me."

Vance spoke up, "I am not here to save you." He said it slowly but in a deeper tone than he normally talks. Bending down to my level.

I shook my head, "Please.""You should have ran away with me. None of this would've happened.""What do you mean, I don't understand you."

"I am a part of the rebellion.""What?""I am the leader of the rebellion."

"What I don't understand. My head hurts.""You will. Victor isn't fit to run his kingdom. I am! Victor only became king because he was the only one in the room when the old king died. Who knows who the old king picked to be king after him! It should've been me!"

Vance stood up, then paced back and forth talking. Most of what he said I didn't understand. My head still hurts.

Vance stopped walking, then bent down to my level on the ground, "Are you listening?!" He screamed in my face.

"Yes.""Will you join me and overthrow my brother? Then you will become my queen."

His face lit up when he said, "my queen." I was silent for a moment. I didn't say anything to him. Is he serious? Why would he do this?

"No. Why?""Why What? Victor was never supposed to be king. He should've died on the battlefield with his men. The night became king. Many knights that we served with died. I almost died."

I looked at him and I realized, "You are jealous of what your brother has.""Yes. I am. With his castle, his servants, his knights, his slave and you. He has you. I heard him go on and on about you. You saved him."

Vance moved closer to me, "You should've saved me on the battlefield. It should've been me, you saved in your family's barn!""I just saw someone that needed my help."

"I need your help.""To overthrow your brother. Your king? No I won't."

Vance shook his head, "What loyalty do you have to him? You ran away many times? I have saved you. He hasn't.""I am loyal to whoever wears the crown. I was taught to be."

Vance pulled on my dress to pull me in closer to him, "Do you love him?""No."

"I can see you blushing. You do love him.""No I don't!"

My face started to blush and red, Vance pulled me closer to him. He kissed me, "I love you.""No you don't. You want me because he has me.""What!"

Vance pulled me away from the wooden beam behind my back and pushed me onto the ground. He laid his hands around my neck and squeezed, starting to choke me.

With every kick he kept squeezing tighter around my neck. He looked like he was getting pleasure from hurting me. As his pleasure increased from choking me, so did his grip, my eyes closed.

My hands are still tied behind my back. I try to move away, but I can't. I tried to kick Vance but Vance moved his body in between my legs.

Now I am starting to panic is Vance going to rape me like Victor? Could both of them be so cruel to me?

"Please stop this!"

He licked my neck then my collarbone, "Maybe I should treat you like Victor then you'll love me." "Please don't!" He rips the bottom of my dress, then I gasped. I tried to kick him off of me. I even tried to roll over to my side. Then maybe I can get up then get away from him.

He just pushed me back down to the ground. For a moment he stopped to look at me, "Please don't do this. I beg you. Please don't be like Victor."

It seemed like when I mentioned Victor's name, it angered him. He rips the top of my dress exposing my breast. His mouth went straight to my right nipple. His tongue flicked on my nipple.

I moaned shamelessly, while arching my back, to have his mouth on my breast fully. He did the same with my right breast, while cupping my other breast in his palm and flicking the nipple with his thumb. He pinched my nipple gently and I let out a gasp.

Victor has taught my body to experience the excitement of sex, "Please stop Vance! I don't want this!" "Your body is telling me something different."

Vance smirked, pulling down his pants. I screamed as loud as I could, "I'm pregnant!"

"What?"

He stopped what he was about to do to me. He pulled up his pants and stood up. I pant, trying to catch my breath.

"Is it true?""Yes."

Still laying down on the ground with my hands still tied behind my back. He paced back and forth, he stopped then turned to me. He started to kick me in my stomach and back, chest everywhere he could.

Vance stopped. I have blood coming from my mouth, my nose, and my lip is bleeding. I am hurting everywhere, Vance turned to me. "I will finish IN you, in front of Victor."

He yelled for his men to come into the room, "Tie her onto my horse. It's time. We ride to the castle."

Vance came back around to face me, "You are my prey."

Now I see the truth about Vance. He is no hero or a good guy. He almost raped me and he beat me. I think if he didn't want Victor to see him rape me then, he would've killed me right there.

Chapter 23

Brother Against Brother

Unknown POV

Vance and the rebels storm the castle. King Victor's and King's Leo fight to the death to protect the kingdom. Blood everywhere, townspeople screaming, fires are blazing in different parts of the kingdom, even the town. Some places are hit worse than others. Townspeople killing each other for food, money, etc. the whole kingdom is divided. Our kingdom desperately needs to believe in, we can rebuild.

Townspeople said that Ivy had been seen tied up on Vance's horse with her mouth covered, when they rode through the town. Her dress is ripped, and she's dirty with hay in her hair; even dirt in her face. She tried to wiggle away, but she still tied up. She tried to scream out for help for anyone to help her. Each time Vance would smack her across the face. Then if someone did try to help, the rebels would kill the town men on spot, without mercy.

Ivy's POV

The truth is I have no idea if I am pregnant or not with Victor's baby. I know what Vance was about to do to me. I didn't want Victor and Vance to both rape me. It's bad enough that Victor does.

For a moment I truly thought he was still going too. As we get closer to the castle, what is he going to do to me? Will he rape me in front of Victor?

I truly thought that Vance was a good person. I look around and see the destruction that Vance and his men are doing. This will not turn out good for anyone.

Vance and his men are storming the castle. Vance still has me hostage. I tried wiggling out of these ropes, but they are too tight and hurting my wrist. Vance is pulling me along. When I stop or close down, Vance pulls my hair and slaps me across the face to walk faster.

His men are fighting Victor's knights and another set of knights, I don't know whom they belong to. I don't think Victor has a knighthood of secret knights. He would probably have already told me about it or I would've found out about it before all of this.

I closed my eyes from seeing the blood everywhere, on the carpets, walls and the dead bodies. Vance still pulled me throughout the castle's hallways to get to where Victor is. I know that's where we are headed too.

***

Victor and King Leo are standing around the feast table. They have moved the table to the middle of the room, the table has maps and paper on the table. It looks like both of them are trying to come up with a battle strategy to fight off the rebels, to end this rebellion. From the look of it, Victor needs all the help he can get.

We walked in immediately Victor's and King Leo's knights started to fight off Vance's men. When Victor saw me, he headed towards me. With my mouth covered up with the cloth I can't say anything. Also, with my hands tied up, I can't say anything.

Vance pulled out his sword, pointing it at Victor. Victor looked shocked, he didn't know what to say or do. He wasn't expecting Victor to be the leader of the rebellion against him.

"Vance, it is true. I didn't want to believe it but it's true. You are the leader of the rebellion."

"Yes, you always have everything handed to you. I was always your shadow."

Victor tried to come over to me, Vance pulled his sword to my neck. I can feel the coldness of the blade. One tear came down my cheeks and onto the blade.

"No you don't touch her."

Vance moved me further away from Victor, "Do you know she's pregnant with your baby?"

The expression on his face changed and his eyes got big, and then he stared at my stomach. Vance watched his eyes go to my stomach. Vance lowered his sword to my stomach.

"Order your men out of this room and Leo's men."

All the knights fighting behind us. Victor didn't think about it, he motioned his men to stop what they were doing.

King Leo yelled out, "Everyone will fight outside these walls."

There men did what they were told to do. No one dropped their weapons, they just backed out of the wooden doors. After shutting the wooden doors, you could hear them fighting. Knights crying out after getting hurt.

Victor, Vance and King Leo and me were left standing in the room, "Now let her go. I did what you asked."

Vance pulled the sword closer to my stomach, then licked my neck, "Maybe I should rape her in front of you."

"No this should be only one on one. Let her go!"

Victor quickly turned around and grabbed his sword off the table, then pointing it at Victor, "I know you don't want to hurt her, you want to hurt me. Come and get it, I'm open."

Victor opens his arms still holding onto the sword in his right hand. Vance pushed away from him, I fell on the ground. I scooted away from Vance. Vance didn't seem to care that I scooted away from him.

King Leo dropped to his knees and helped remove the cloth away from my mouth. Vance seemed to care that King Leo was in the room or not. Or even helping me with the ropes.

Both Victor and Vance holding their swords in their hands and pointing at each other. Each time one of the moves then the other brother would try to make a move. Trying to get the first blow. But every time they did, the other brother's sword would stop the blow by whipping around and all you could see and hear clashing steel.

***

King Leo tried as quickly as he could to help take off ropes around my wrist, "Can't you help him?"

"This is out of my hands. This time is brother against brother."

Victor closes the distance with a sword raised preparing for what appears to be a mighty overhead strike. With Vance's sword still raised, he makes a hard kick to midsection.

Victor cry's out in pain, while Vance quickly takes the chance to raise his sword to intercept against Victor's sword. You hear clashing steel.

"This kingdom is mine! You don't deserve it!"

"And you think you do?"

"Name one thing you did right for this kingdom!"

Victor steps towards Vance, and prepares to deliver a full force overhead attack on Vance with speed and intent. Vance wisely parries the attack with the forte (the strongest part) of his sword.

"I stopped the war!"

"With my help! You wouldn't have stopped the war if it wasn't for my help. The knighthood didn't see you as their king."

Without missing a beat, Victor follows up with what looks like the same attack that Vance tried to do to him, however..

"They respect me!"

"It's because I did first then they followed my lead! You couldn't have all of this if it wasn't for me!"

While Victor is looking at Vance's head and keeping the actual target only in his peripheral vision, he sidesteps out of the way of any potential counterattack and attacks with one hand, suddenly dropping the attack into Vance's foremost leg. Vance drops his sword and falls to the ground in pain. Blood coming from where the sword cut his leg.

"No, I earned where I am at with blood, sweat and tears! No one is going to take this away from me! You may look at it that way, but I know the truth and what you said is far away from the truth!"

Blood is all over the floor now. Victor pointed the sword to Vance's throat, "You can't do it, can you?"

The truth is Victor couldn't. Traitor or not, Vance was still his brother after all. Blood brothers. He can't break that bond.

"You can't but I can!" With all of his might, Vance grabbed his sword and lunged at Victor. Stabbing Victor on the left side of his stomach.

Victor falls to the ground coughing up blood.

"No!!"

I screamed out, and I tugged on the ropes with my teeth and I broke out of my ropes. With full force I ran into Vance, and he lost his balance, he fell out the open windows.

I just stood there. What did I just do?

King Leo ran to Victor helping him up, then King Leo, Victor and I, we looked down and saw outside the window. Vance is dead on the ground. He broke his neck and leg. He fell out the window of a three-floor window. Vance died immediately. Blood coming from the ground under him, where his head is.

King Leo, Victor and I looked at each other. We knew the rebellion was over.

The End

CPSIA information can be obtained
at www.ICGtesting.com
Printed in the USA
LVHW080636271222
735871LV00009B/471